The Merman

by

Kathy Sharp

All rights reserved, no part of this publication may be reproduced or transmitted by any means whatsoever
without the prior permission of the publisher.

Additional editing by Fi Woods

Cover image by Diane Narraway

ISBN: 978-1-916756-03-8

VENEFICIA PUBLICATIONS UK

August 2023

veneficiapublications.com

CONTENTS

1: All Washed Up	1
2: The Old Castle	12
3: A Fish in a Frock Coat	24
4: The Buckled Bell	31
5: The Hatchet-Faced Man	44
6: Spats in the Belfry	54
7: The Ship of the Sky	62
8: A Different Degree of Oddness	72
9: The Scarlet Woman	79
10: The Sea Whisperer	88
11: Master Delphinus	94
12: The Suit of Yellow	103
13: Bell, Book, and Cannon	113
14: Message on a Bottom	125
15: A Glut of Guardians	132
16: Barnacles Speak Louder Than Words	148
Epilogue	158

All Washed Up

People ran screaming from the apparition. 'It is a merman, come to steal our children!'

'Eh?' said the Reverend Pontius, almost knocked off his feet by the onrush. 'What?'

'A merman! We have displeased the Spirit of the Sea, and he has sent this punishment!'

The Reverend retrieved his hat from the oily puddle it had landed in when he was barged out of the way. It was his best Sunday hat, too. This was where the fish barrels stood, and every puddle contained essence of mackerel, and, in this heat, the smell would be with him for many Sundays to come, he thought.

'Reverend, you will not be safe! You must run!'

'Nonsense. I'll do no such thing.' Pontius was thinking that he wasn't as young as he used to be, and his running days were probably over anyway. Being told to run for his life had been a not uncommon experience through the years he had spent on the Isle of Larus. These people saw something they didn't understand and reacted with panic. Usually, for no really good reason. So, what was it that had scared them all *this* time?

'Show me,' he said. Pontius had found that it generally paid to keep questions as short and direct as possible.

'It is dangerous Reverend, sir.'

'I'll be the judge of that,' said Pontius, testily. It was sure to be nothing, as usual. 'Now, what is it?'

A chorus of fingers pointed at the harbour. 'What?' said Pontius, peering. 'You mean that? It's a boat.'

'Oh, sir, not just a boat!'

But it was. A small boat drifting in towards the quay.

'It is a merman's boat!'

'How d'ye know that?' snapped Pontius, and then rolled his eyes, awaiting the obvious answer.

'There is a merman in it, sir.'

'Preposterous. There is no such thing.' It was out before he could stop himself. Pontius had learned over time that it was unwise to utter the phrase, "there is no such thing", because the moment you did, the thing in question had a nasty habit of appearing. It was a feature of life on the Isle of Larus.

People shook their heads. The Reverend was a brave gentleman, they knew. Altogether too brave at times. Foolhardy. Especially when their own eyes told them there was a merman, large as life, in that there boat.

'Look, sir. He has a fish tail! All white ...'

'It's a bit of sailcloth wrapped round him, that's all ...'

'But he has a merman's beard, growing like seaweed from his chin ...'

'It *is* seaweed. I'm quite sure it comes off ... Give me that thing.' Pontius pointed to the long boathook someone had brought to fight off the merman. The boat was just below them now, bumping the quay. Pontius leaned over and put the hook under the seaweed. It came away.

'Oh, he has taken off the merman's beard!'

'It's not a beard: it's seaweed. *Look.*' He heaved the seaweed onto the quay, where it fell with a splat.

'That is a mortal man. We must help him.'

It was indeed a perfectly ordinary man. Dead or alive, Pontius couldn't tell. Deathly pale. At least, he thought, if he's beyond help we can give him a decent burial. That's if I can persuade these fools that he isn't a merman.

'Will somebody *please* help me secure the boat, so I can tend to him?' There was no response.

Pontius fumed in silence. How could he persuade them to help him?

'I'll play them at their own game,' he muttered.

'Listen. This man is clearly a gift from the Spirit of the Sea. Will you not help him? The Spirit will be truly displeased if you reject this gift, don't you think?'

He had hit the right note, and Ligo the fisherman, big gangling fellow that he was, came forward.

'*I* will help the Rev'rend; not wishin' to offend the Spirit,' he said. But he didn't look too sure. 'What shall I do, sir?'

Really, thought Pontius, these folks live every day of their lives with boats and they want *me* to tell them what to do. He would have to give them step-by-step instructions, or he would be left on the quay all day, holding the boathook. He tried to put a note of authority into his voice.

'Master Ligo. Thank you. Would you go and find another small boat, if you please, and bring it here. Attach it ... er ... with a rope, to this boat. Then tow this one round to the little shingle beach and pull it ashore. Can you do that for me?'

Ligo looked doubtful but pulled himself together.

'Fetch another boat; hook on a tow rope; beach the merman's boat on the shingle. Is that right?'

'Absolutely,' said Pontius. 'Good man. I knew I could rely upon you, young sir.' He was painfully aware that the poor fellow in the boat might be expiring while this conversation went on, but there was no hurrying the people of Larus.

'Would it be convenient for you to begin now? I will meet you on the beach, and we'll see what's to be done.'

Ligo preened himself at Pontius' first remark and looked doubtful again at the second. But in the end, he loped off to find a boat.

'Shouldn't we call Rufus the Hermit?' somebody asked.

This was a fair question. Rufus, the Isle's western guardian, certainly counted as their representative regarding the Spirit of the Sea.

'He won't come down,' Pontius said. 'You know that. But it would be courteous to send someone up to inform him of these latest developments—don't you think?'

This seemed to satisfy everyone, and a volunteer set off for the west cliff to tell Rufus all about it.

'And don't exaggerate!' Pontius called after him. Stories tended to be embroidered in the telling on Larus.

'Now, let us see what we can do to help this poor gentleman, if anything.' Pontius did wonder if he might regret calling him a "gift from the sea", but that would have to wait. 'Can somebody bring me a flask of water?'

'Is you feeling faint, Reverend?' someone asked.

Pontius was losing patience.

'It's not for me, you idiot; it's for the merman. I mean the man in the boat. Bring it down to the beach. I need to get there before Master Ligo does.'

It seemed to take an interminable time, but at last the boat was retrieved and beached. 'Bah,' said Pontius to himself, as he waited, 'they are a lot of sheep.'

'Bah! Oh, very clever,' said somebody, behind their hands.

Others were still muttering 'merman' and calling out warnings to the Reverend to beware: mermen had sharp teeth and the bite would turn anyone on the receiving end into mermen, too. Have a care, Reverend, and keep away from the biting end.

Pontius huffed and rattled down the shingle for a proper look. He peered over the gunwale; the braver islanders following. The man in the boat looked dead, but he *did* have a reassuring lack of fins and tail.

'There,' said Pontius, 'a mortal man, just as I said. Now, let's hear no more of this "merman" nonsense.'

He leaned down and gently put the back of his hand to the man's dead-white, clammy forehead. The eyes snapped open. Pontius was taken so much by surprise that he leapt back, overbalanced, and collapsed on the shingle. By the time he had managed to sit up and feel about for injuries, there wasn't a soul left on the beach, beyond himself. Master Ligo, now returning his borrowed boat, and a little way offshore, had stopped and was leaning on his oars with a look of concern.

'Rev'rend! Are you injured?' he called. 'Did the merman bite you at all?'

'No,' yelled Pontius, brushing himself down. 'I am perfectly well.' He could feel a set of shingle-shaped bruises forming on his elbow. 'He is not a merman—he is a poor mariner come to some harm. Will you come ashore and assist me, Master Ligo?'

Pontius leaned again over the gunwale, his heart thumping. Ridiculous, he thought, this person is not in a fit state to attack anyone.

'Good morning, sir. *Ahem*, I am the Reverend Pontius, Eastern Guardian, Isle of Larus,' he said, feeling something formal was called for. There was no response. 'That is where you are, you see. Larus.' he added.

The merman opened his mouth and croaked, '*Aaargh.*'

'Having a bit o' trouble with his gills I 'spect, Reverend.' said Ligo, now ashore and peering fearfully across from the other side of the boat.

'Nonsense,' said Pontius, 'he hasn't got any gills … look.'

'Water,' groaned the merman.

'Of course. Just one moment, sir, and I shall bring you some.' That came out sounding like the answer of a potboy in a tavern. Pontius found the water flask abandoned on the shingle and took it to the boat.

'You're sure he's not a merman?' said Ligo.

Pontius rolled his eyes.

'Would a merman be in need of water? Here, Master Ligo ... lift him ... prop him up, so I can give him some water.'

Ligo gingerly leaned into the beached boat and lifted the man.

'Water,' croaked the merman again, and Ligo nearly dropped him.

'Here, sir,' said Pontius soothingly, 'very fresh water from our well.'

He put the flask to the merman's dry lips and he drank greedily, before collapsing back. It had been too much effort. Ligo and Pontius exchanged glances across the boat. Too soon to say if he would live or die.

The little crowd had come out of hiding and were lurking at a safe distance.

'Well, don't just stand there,' Pontius called to them, 'fetch a blanket and find somewhere we can take him indoors.' They hovered a moment, like a flock of sheep, undecided which direction to take.

'Now!' bellowed Pontius, and they fled.

'We'll take you somewhere more comfortable shortly, sir.' said Pontius.

'Castello.' croaked the merman.

'What's a "castello", Reverend?' asked Ligo.

'I believe it might be his name, Master Ligo.'

The Old Castle

'Mind my hat,' called the Reverend Pontius who was having trouble keeping up. He had set it on the man's sun-scorched face, just to provide a little shade, and then had to explain that no, the merman wasn't dead, and could they just get on, please.

There was only one room remaining of the old castle. It was shabby, moth-eaten, and often damp, but, for now, it was indoors and out of the fierce sun. They carried Castello into the cool of its walls and he was asleep before they had set up a cot for him.

'Sleep will restore him,' said the Reverend Pontius. 'I shall come in and attend to him every few hours. He will do very well.'

The Reverend sincerely hoped he was right in this prediction. People seemed to expect him to pontificate on such matters and, over the years, he had learned to do it with a certain confidence, though he never quite trusted his own judgement. The islanders did, however. If the Reverend says the fellow will live, then he will live. Simple as that. Oh, that I had such faith, Pontius thought privately.

There was a vague plan to move the merman somewhere more comfortable as soon as he recovered a little.

'For the umpteenth time: he is *not* a merman,' Pontius had said in exasperation, 'See: he has feet, like everyone else.' But a legend, once established on Larus, was very hard to shift—however clear the evidence against it might be. Pontius had encouraged them to call the man by his name, "Castello", but they clung stubbornly to the legend and, at best, called him "Castello the Merman". Pontius supposed that was at least half-right and said no more. They would drop the merman part once they saw the man walking about on ordinary feet—not fins—but that wouldn't be for a while. The poor fellow was still prostrated from lying for goodness-knows-how-long in an open boat, in broiling heat. After initially recovering a little, he was showing definite signs of delirium, which worried the Reverend.

No one would touch the ship's boat left deserted on the beach.

'Surely,' Pontius said, 'someone can make use of it? It would be helpful to have an extra boat for use in the harbour, would it not? Or for inshore fishing, crab-pots and whatnot?' The Reverend did his best to hide his considerable ignorance of these matters, even after so many years' residence in a fishing community. People stared at him. Had he said the wrong thing?

'But it is the merman's boat,' somebody said at last. 'It's not for us to interfere with it. He will want it back.'

Pontius resisted the urge to stamp his foot and assert for the millionth time that Castello was *not* a merman. But what would be the point? They had got it into their heads. I must be more wily than that, he thought, and tried another tack.

'The merman has told me himself that it is not *his* boat; it was simply his means of coming to Larus.' Castello had said no such thing, or much at all, in fact, but Pontius hoped they didn't know that.

'He says it was provided for him by the Spirit of the Sea: a gift in his hour of need. It has served its purpose in bringing him here, and he has no further use for it.'

Castello hadn't said that, either, but he had regained consciousness for long enough, at one point, to say that he was "*very* glad indeed to see the back of the thing." Pontius concluded from this that Castello was unlikely to want the boat in the immediate future and he did hate to see anything going needlessly to waste, so he pressed on. 'I don't think that the Spirit would appreciate his generous gift being left to rot on the beach. It is a gift for all of us, not just the merman. It would be churlish to refuse it, wouldn't you say?'

Heads were beginning to nod.

'The Reverend is wise,' said Ligo, the fisherman. 'I'll go and find some oars.'

Pontius mopped his brow. He thought he had probably won that particular battle, but he would need to watch them like a hawk to ensure they didn't just hide the boat out of his sight.

And then ... well ... the weather broke; broke into thundery gushes and downpours. There was no moving the merman until it all dried up.

Ah! Such rain. To begin with, the islanders were grateful and gave thanks to the Spirit of the Sea for the replenishment of the wells. The Reverend Pontius suggested they might aim some of their gratitude at the Spirit of the Sky. After all, that's where all the precious water was coming from.

Out of politeness to the Reverend, some of them complied. In private, though, they said that they had always had plenty of weather before he brought *that* spirit, *his* spirit, to their attention, and continued to worship the Spirit of the Sea regardless.

But after a few days of this extraordinary bounty everyone was feeling that this was enough; thank you all the same. The island was overflowing with new streams forming waterfalls over the cliffs and running down the steep hill to the harbour. People who lived on the steepest parts and at the bottom took to opening both front and back doors, and allowing the water to gush in one side and out the other. It was generally less bother than trying to prevent the ingress of the water.

Now and then, household items carelessly left in the way of the flood were picked up and carried down the hill with the deluge. The Reverend Pontius, squelching daily up and down the hill in a tolerably waterproof tarpaulin cloak, remarked at the way these pots, pans, stools, and baskets always found their way back to their proper owners. Nothing, he said, ever seemed to be surreptitiously snatched or misappropriated.

'Why, sir,' people said, speaking as if to an idiot, 'this is a very small isle, as you will have noticed and everyone on it knows what everyone else has in their houses. What use would it be to go taking someone else's things when we'd all know who they belonged to, and who'd taken them? Don't make no sense, sir.'

This excellent logic had shut Pontius up abruptly. His youthful experience of the wider world—now fading far into the past, but not forgotten—told him that theft was not so easily prevented elsewhere. But who was he to break this unpleasant news to the islanders?

'Not I,' he muttered, tipping the rainwater out of his hat, and squelching off down the hill for the umpteenth time to see how Castello was faring. In recent days he had spent more time traipsing up and down, from his chapel on the top of the island to the old castle by the quay, than doing anything else. His lessons for the island children had gone untaught, sermons had remained unwritten, and preaching had remained unpreached. No one had complained and Pontius had thought at first that this was a sign of concern for Castello. Everyone seemed so relentlessly jolly, though, that he began to suspect they actually enjoyed the lack of schooling and spiritual activities.

'Just as soon as the weather improves,' he said, 'I'll get them to carry him up to the chapel. Then I can watch him and tend to my work, too.'

Each night during that time of wet weather, Reverend Pontius sat up with his patient. He liked to think of him that way, rather than as a recipient of mere pastoral care. Besides, no one else would do it—what with him being a merman.

The Reverend thought that the sound of a human voice might be soothing to the poor man, and he kept up a one-sided conversation on any subject that came to mind.

'I had thought at one time,' he murmured, 'to found a college—an academy—here on Larus. It was an idea that amused me for some time. Not a theological institution, you understand.' He was anticipating the question Castello might have asked, had he heard a word of it.

'No, a more general sort of college for young people to expand their minds. A charitable institution.' Pontius settled himself more comfortably in his creaky chair.

'I had so much enjoyed teaching the people here their letters—and many other things about the wider world, so far as I could—I thought it a suitable enterprise for a man of the cloth. That was in my younger days, of course. I had the audacity to imagine it as *The Pontius College, Isle of Larus*. It lived a great while in my mind, as an admired centre of learning: a place to which people would flock, you see. Put the Isle of Larus on the map—and me with it—if I am entirely honest.

Of course, you will laugh, sir, at my foolishness. My grand plans did not take account of the costs and difficulties of such an undertaking. I should have needed a wealthy patron and they are a little thin on the ground in these parts, as you can imagine. Youthful pride and arrogance got the better of me. Oh, the follies of youth, sir! In the end, though, I confess that it wasn't the practical difficulties that made me abandon the idea. No—but, oh, when I thought of the things that might follow if I should succeed in putting Larus *on the map*—I liked them not at all. I decided that it was far better left *off* the map, since I love it just as it is. Perhaps you think that a selfish notion, sir? Perhaps it is.'

Pontius seemed to have overlooked the fact that the self-aggrandisement of a college bearing his own name might be an even more selfish notion. But whether it was or it wasn't was immaterial, for Castello hadn't heard a syllable of it, and the Reverend himself had dozed off in his chair long before he could think it through.

Something made Pontius shift in his less than comfortable seat and wake from his doze.

'Just resting my eyes,' he muttered, 'not asleep.'

He had been sure for a moment that someone was there—but no—it was just himself and the unconscious Castello.

The Reverend stretched, easing out the cramps in his knees. It was already daylight outside, despite the pouring rain. Perhaps a fisherman was about: they were a hardy people on Larus, the Reverend thought, still not quite awake.

He got up and walked stiffly to the small window, which was letting in a beam of damp and murky light. And then he saw it. Words had been written in the raindrops.

"We shall set him three tasks" it read. Pontius almost fell backwards. Many years ago, he had found a message written in the frost on a window. Indeed, it had brought him to Larus. Now here was another. The rainwater dribbling on the ancient glass pane obscured the message as he stared at it, and then washed it clean away. Was this something he should take seriously? Or somebody's idea of a joke? He felt in his bones it was serious.

'But *who* ... *who* exactly is "*we*"?' he murmured. '*Me*? The *Spirit*? A multiplicity of spirits?' It made his head swim to think about it. 'And tasks for ...

our merman? Let us hope he lives to see them.'

But the message hadn't finished. Fresh words appeared on the pane.

"One for the Isle, one for a friend, one for himself," Pontius mouthed.

There was certainly nobody there. Just himself and the words, again washing away on the window. It was a message clearly meant for Pontius.

And just what form might these tasks take, he wondered, looking at Castello's sleeping form. At all events, he would not be mentioning this to anyone else.

A Fish in a Frock Coat

When the rain eventually stopped and the sticky heat returned, they carried the merman, sailor-style in an old hammock, all the way up the steep hill from the harbour to the top of the Isle. All in this clammy, still heat, too, with one of the ladies having lent a salt-battered parasol to keep the sun off Castello's equally salt-battered face.

The Reverend Pontius, in charge of the parasol, walked with them, mopping his brow with his third-best threadbare handkerchief.

He had asked if they couldn't leave this transportation until a cooler time of day but hadn't been much surprised when they turned on him in astonishment. Did the Reverend not know of the especially favourable fishing conditions that would certainly occur that afternoon? Pontius muttered irritably that it must have slipped his mind, while they rolled their eyes affectionately. No, it must be done now, or wait. Fishing would always come first. So Pontius had agreed, despite it turning so warm. The constant trailing up and down the hill to attend to Castello was beginning to have unpleasant effects on the Reverend's knees.

'Very well,' he had said testily, 'let us get it done; once and for all.'

So up they had gone, everyone chatting merrily, with frequent stops to let the Reverend get his breath back. At the top of the hill they caught a pleasant breeze, and Pontius was happier as they crossed the grassy flats on the island top, heading for the chapel.

Once in its cool interior, they set up a truckle-bed for the invalid in Pontius' living quarters under the belltower. The two of them were left in peace, aside from frequent interruptions from the island women bringing broth or balm, or entirely unnecessary extra blankets.

'At least I need not tramp up and down that damnable hill every five minutes,' muttered Pontius, as he busied himself.

'Excuse the language, if you please.' This remark was accompanied by an upward glance and addressed, not to Castello, who was unconscious anyway, but to the Spirit of the Sky. In any case, the Spirit was apparently otherwise engaged or simply not listening, and Pontius concluded that walking all the way up that hill, in that heat, holding a parasol was sufficiently good a deed to cancel out a bit of minor swearing.

'How is your merman, Reverend?' How many more times were they going to ask, Pontius wondered. The interruptions had been ceaseless, and any chance of catching up on the unwritten sermons had been lost.

'The merman ...' Pontius stopped himself. 'That is, Master Castello, is resting. I shall stay with him, but I beg you all to leave him in peace while he recovers.'

If he recovers, Pontius thought, as he went back into the chapel.

Castello was unconscious, but uneasy, muttering to himself. Pontius recognised this as delirium, as he had feared, and immediately found himself in a moral quandary. People said all kinds of things—unwise things, secret things—in delirium. Things they wouldn't dream of saying aloud in other circumstances. So, was it right or fair to listen to them? Castello was muttering, mouthing words quietly, and it would be necessary for Pontius to lean in close to hear properly. He was torn: this was akin to reading someone's private journal, wasn't it? An unforgivable intrusion—and yet, if he did not listen, he might miss the last request of a dying man. Pontius was a man of the cloth, after all; it was his duty to attend the gravely ill, to hear their final words and provide what spiritual comfort he could. And he couldn't do that if he put his fingers in his ears and refused to listen.

Was it best to listen, then? Nothing said would be repeated, after all. But, oh, supposing the man confessed to some frightful crime?

Pontius had attended the dying on many occasions, but their final words had invariably been inconsequential. It was surprising how many people made last-minute enquiries about the weather, or complaints about the catering. The most striking deathbed remark he had heard on Larus was from an aged lady who had gripped his arm with surprising strength and said urgently, 'Please see that my feather pillow goes to my great-nephew and none other,' before expiring on the self-same pillow. Pontius had seen that her wishes were carried out, though he'd privately observed that he wouldn't much have wanted the pillow himself, given its recent history.

But this was different: to begin with, it was uncertain whether Castello would die or not, and furthermore, Pontius had no idea at all of the man's history. Why, he *could* be a pirate, coming from the sea in a ship's boat as he had. Who could say what ghastly crimes he might have committed? Or maybe none at all. Pontius shrugged.

In the end, he let his curiosity get the better of him and listened in. But, as it happened, most of Castello's mutterings made no sense whatsoever. Pontius didn't know whether to be relieved or disappointed. He had hoped he might learn *something* about him.

On the one occasion the patient did make sense, he seemed to mistake the cool gloom of the chapel for the depths of the ocean.

'So, I am drowned.' he had murmured to Pontius' waiting ear. 'The seabed is not so comfortable as I had expected ... very lumpy.'

Pontius thought it a little ungracious to complain about the accommodations, even for someone who thought himself drowned. He got up to stretch his legs a little.

'Oh, I am drowned,' said Castello again, opening his eyes wide and staring at Pontius.

'Why, there is a very stout and ungainly fish in a frock coat swimming by.'

Pontius chuckled, realising the "fish in a frock coat" referred to himself moving about the room. The delirium must be very great, he thought. After all, how could anyone see *him*—such a fine figure of a man—as stout and ungainly?

The Buckled Bell

Captain Castello awoke from a long sleep in and out of delirium and said, 'What bird?' At least, he thought he had said it. The nature of reality had been a sad puzzle to him for some time.

'What bird?' he said again, mainly to test his voice. He thought he heard himself and was more than a little surprised when he received an answer.

'The singing bird? Oh, I believe they call it a robin.' This was the Reverend Pontius, sitting at the bedside and yawning.

'We do not have many songbirds here on Larus ... except in spring and autumn, when they seem to pass through in flocks ... but not otherwise,' he added sleepily.

'Ah. Indeed,' said Castello. He was listening to the sad-toned singing. It had been his constant companion, weaving its way through the many curious dreams that had afflicted him. He had fancied himself at sea, and the ship sang to him; he was eating a meal of chicken and finding his dinner serenading him; he had thought himself in a forest and the very leaves on the trees had grown mouths and warbled at him. All very strange and yet steady, reliable, and comforting: that birdsong had been the only predictable thing in a most disturbing world. And now it had a name: robin.

Pontius, unaware of all this, was pleased that the Captain had asked a logical question. It was an encouraging sign of recovery after all the gibberish of delirium. Most satisfactory. He turned to say something to Castello but found he had fallen back asleep. I should enquire, thought Pontius, more than half-asleep himself, why the birds come in spring and autumn like that. Where do they go, I wonder? Why do they not stay in the same places? It would be an interesting line of enquiry when he had a moment to himself. Natural philosophy was considered a suitable occupation for men of the cloth, after all. I must pursue the study of it, he thought, and dozed off where he sat. The robin, settled in its usual place on the scrubby elder bush outside the window, sang on and entertained no ideas at all of pursuing the study of the Reverend Pontius.

'Are you able to talk now, sir?' Pontius spoke quietly to the invalid, now awake. The man had slept peacefully for a good while. Pontius was no physician, but he felt it had been touch-and-go with their merman. I must stop calling him that, Pontius thought. It's the kind of thing that sets off ridiculous rumours among the people, and once they get these ideas into their heads it's impossible to winkle them out again. We shall have merman rumours until the very end of time, you may depend upon it. So, I must set the pace by calling him Master Castello, if he will only confirm that is truly his name.

There was no time like the present, Pontius thought, so he tried again.

'Are you feeling better, Master Castello? More yourself now?' Pontius fussed around, plumping pillows and clearing away dishes.

Castello looked at him—still a little stupid, if truth be told—and said, 'I do not know, sir.'

Pontius couldn't help an impatient cluck. Surely the man must know whether he felt better or not.

'Well, sir,' he said, 'you have a better colour today and your salt sores are healing. I deduce you must feel better for that.'

'I suppose I must, sir, but as to feeling more like myself, I cannot tell.'

Pontius felt another stab of impatience—why couldn't the fellow just say "yes, thank you", like anybody else?

'What I mean to say is, I have no idea what myself is.'

'*Eh?*' Pontius had to restrain himself from rolling his eyes.

'I am bemusing you, sir, and I apologise,' said Castello. 'What I am trying to say is that I have no memory of my former life, or of how I came to be here.'

'Oh.' Pontius felt another stab: disappointment this time. He had so been looking forward to hearing news of the outside world. Boats from the mainland had become increasingly irregular in recent years and sailors' yarns were not to be taken too seriously, anyway. Here, at last, was someone gentlemanly—someone Pontius hoped he could speak to as an equal. There was so much world beyond Larus, and he knew so little of it these days. And now it seemed the man had no recollections, no knowledge—nothing to discuss at all. It was a crushing disappointment.

Unwilling to give up, Pontius tried again.

'Come now, sir. Do you remember nothing at all?'

'Well, there is something ...'

'Yes?' said Pontius encouragingly, a stab of hope cutting through the disappointment.

'Well, I know I am *Captain* Castello, not Master Castello.'

'Oh.' Disappointment won the day, fair and square.

'Well, *Captain*, I am all apologies. I wish you a full recovery very shortly.' Pontius prepared to leave and got as far as the door, before a thought struck him. 'And by the way, I am the *Reverend* Pontius, since we are talking titles.'

That told him, Pontius thought, as he went on his way.

He was halfway down the hill before he realised he had stormed out of his own chapel.

Needless to say, the Reverend quickly regretted this ill-tempered exchange. He was among friends on Larus and had felt so since his arrival, many years before. He was *among* friends, but he didn't *have* a friend. Not a particular friend, with whom he had things in common. He liked the people of Larus—loved them even—for their unaffected ways, their simplicity, their kindness, their honesty. But a *real* friend: someone he could truly talk to and who would understand the sheer strangeness of life on the Isle of Larus had not appeared. Until now. And he had ruined it all with ridiculous temper and rudeness. It was a punishment from the Spirit of the Sky, that this longed-for friend should be snatched away by Pontius' own stupidity.

To tell the truth, he was greatly impressed too, by the title of "captain". A sea captain, was he? A person of standing and influence? Pontius so wanted to know more. A *captain*, even one who had lost his memory, would feel like an ally. And in the course of polite and interesting conversations (Pontius flattered himself) surely that memory would begin to return a little.

No, Pontius thought, I must swallow my pride, go back to him, and apologise; and there is no time like the present. So back he went, head down into the wind, wondering exactly what he should say to put things right.

He plunged straight in and told the truth.

'Captain Castello, I apologise unreservedly, sir, for my ill-temper. I confess I was so looking forward to hearing some news of the outside world that I indulged myself in disappointment when you told me you had no memories to share. That is a serious lapse for a man of the cloth, and I do hope you can forgive me.'

Castello, propped up on his pillows, stared at Pontius sadly.

'And I confess I am equally disappointed at having nothing to share, my dear sir ... Reverend.'

'You are a sea captain then, sir? In charge of a large vessel, perhaps?'

There was a long silence while Castello considered his answer.

'No,' he said at last. 'Captain of artillery.'

'Ah,' said Pontius, 'well, I'm sure that is a position of great responsibility too.'

'To be honest, I scarcely know,' said Castello. 'Perhaps I have suffered an injury to the brain. I remember very little of anything. Except your kindness in tending to me, Reverend.'

This vagueness unsettled the Reverend a little. Could he trust anything this man might say? Was he *really* a captain of artillery? What *was* a captain of artillery, exactly? Pontius knew nothing of armed forces, except that they did exist in some parts of the world. He knew some ships carried guns—he had seen them for himself—but they were mostly carried for protection against pirates, weren't they? Not that anyone he knew of had suffered pirate attacks. It was all largely a thing of the past.

Indeed, there were a couple of rusty, aged cannons down by the old castle, left behind in the long ago. These days they were mostly used by the fishermen, as handy places to drape their nets. And the very room Castello had occupied down there was almost all that was left of a decrepit castle.

'A thing of the past,' said Pontius aloud. But Captain Castello, captain of artillery or not, had fallen asleep again.

When he awoke some hours later, Pontius was still there, making a start on a sermon.

'I do apologise, Reverend,' he said, 'but this sleepiness overcomes me suddenly.'

'No need for apologies, my dear sir,' said Pontius. 'You have been so very ill. Sleep is a great restorative.'

'I hope we may talk of many things,' said Castello, 'and that this will encourage the return of my memory. Perhaps you would indulge me by telling me something of your life on this isle, to begin with? If you can spare the time?'

If he could spare the time!

Of *course* he could. Pontius had just been granted his dearest wish: someone to talk to. He nodded eagerly, took a seat by the invalid, and said, 'Of course, of course. Where would you like me to begin?' The half-written sermon fell to the floor unheeded.

It had been a little disappointing to find that life on the mysterious and distant Isle of Larus had pretty much the same problems and difficulties as anywhere else. The young Reverend Pontius, something of a firebrand, had arrived full of zeal. Well, to tell the truth, he was pretty lukewarm as firebrands go, but he had been anticipating new and interesting challenges on the Isle. Chief among these had been his role as missionary: bringing the Spirit of the

Sky to an island that cheerfully worshipped the Spirit of the Sea. That would surely be difficult, wouldn't it? But no—the islanders of Larus had proved to be so accepting, so very accommodating, that it hadn't been much of a challenge at all.

"Of course," they had said, "no problem at all. Would the Reverend like them to make a little chapel for him? They could build in a little accommodation for him, if he didn't mind living on the premises.". Pontius had been puffed up, ready to argue his point with a list of benefits, but the total lack of opposition, along with the sheer kindness deflated him. He had quite been looking forward to a wrangle, he realised. In fact, there had been very little to argue about in all the years he had spent on Larus.

Pontius had never spoken of this to anyone, and he wasn't at all sure how much of it he could risk revealing to the merman, or Captain Castello, as he must now think of him. It was natural to be cautious with confidences—you never knew where unleashing them might lead—nor how confidential they might remain.

So, in telling his story to the convalescent Captain, Pontius was inclined to stick to the facts rather than reveal the disappointments of his heart.

'So, you see, sir,' he said, 'the people kindly built this chapel for me, all in this very robust stone. It is both my workplace and my home. They even found me an old ship's bell for the tower. It is a little buckled, but it does the job of calling people in to hear the sermons. We ring it occasionally to indicate a shipwreck, too, you see, but that's a rare thing.'

Castello had perked up at the mention of the bell.

'Oh, Reverend,' he said. 'Metalwork! It is something I know about. Don't ask me how I know, but I do. I might be able to unbuckle the bell for you if you'll permit me. Or at least polish it up nicely. Improve the tone, perhaps?'

Pontius was delighted.

'So you shall, my dear sir, as soon as you are recovered. We do have a blacksmith on the Isle, but he hasn't been able to take the buckle out of the bell. I'm sure Master Ferro won't mind if you try; he has more than enough to do attending to the fishing boats' metalwork, without having to mess about with buckled bells. I should be very grateful for your assistance.'

It was a while before it occurred to the Reverend that he had just set Castello a *task*. The words written in the raindrops came back to him: "We shall set him three tasks". Had he, himself, unconsciously just set the first of them? Unbuckling the bell was an odd test to set someone, if test it was, but who was he to question the ways of the spirits? The thought struck him that this was indeed likely to be the work of the Spirit of the Sea—the spirit he didn't officially believe in or acknowledge.

'It's a ship's bell, after all,' he said to himself. 'Of course it comes within that Spirit's jurisdiction.'

The Hatchet-Faced Man

'There is a man with a face like an axe, Mother says,' said the child. 'Your honour, sir,' he added.

Pontius paused, a spoonful of breakfast egg halfway to his mouth. The chapel door was always open to all, including, and especially, messengers.

'A face like a ... what?' he asked. The boy was talking nonsense. 'A face like a ...' The egg slipped off the spoon and slid down the front of the Reverend's clean shirt. 'Oh.'

'That'll not come out,' observed the boy, as Pontius dabbed at it until the bright stain was widely spread.

'Mother says ...'

'Never mind what Mother says.' The Reverend's day was getting off to a bad start.

'Now, what was the message? And keep your voice down.' He glanced at Castello, fast asleep on the makeshift bed in the corner. 'He's still unwell, and I don't want to wake him.'

'Wants to see you,' said the boy, more softly, 'man with a face like an axe. I *think* it was an axe.'

'Nonsense,' said Pontius, still feebly dabbing at the egg stain. 'How can anyone have a face like an axe?'

The boy opened his mouth for another 'Mother says', but Pontius cut him short.

'Tell him I'm coming. Where is he?'

'Quay,' said the child, not one to waste words. 'Boat captain. Just in. Things for sale. Asked for person in charge.' He thrust his hands into his pockets in an annoyingly casual way.

Pontius couldn't resist a tiny smile. It was to be hoped that their southern guardian didn't hear that he, Pontius, had been called upon as the person in charge of the Isle. She'd have an apoplexy. Still, the message had been delivered to him, and he would answer it.

'I've egg on my shirt,' he said, quite unnecessarily. 'I'll be down as soon as I can. Give him that message if you please. And take your hands out of your pockets.'

The boy skipped off, and could be heard chanting, 'I'm to say he has egg on his shirt, and he'll be down as soon as he can,' as he went along.

Pontius had barely rendered himself respectable in a clean shirt when the chapel door burst open revealing Rissa, the ship-warden—the island's southern guardian herself—eye-bogglingly bright in her habitual scarlet gown.

'Reverend, we must go down to the quay.' she said. It was not a request. 'There's a man ...'

'With a face like an axe. I know.' said Pontius irritably. 'I do wish you'd knock, madam, before you come in.'

Rissa ignored the latter remark.

'Really, Reverend, how can anyone have a face like an axe? It's a *hatchet*-faced man; a sea captain asking to see someone in charge. Naturally I am on my way to meet him; I thought you might accompany me.'

The cheek of the woman, Pontius thought, to assume the message was intended for *her*! But he fetched his hat anyway, looked in on the still-asleep Castello—goodness knows how he was still asleep, given all the racket—and shut the door quietly behind himself. And off they went, down the hill to the quay in a state of mutual grumpiness.

The sea captain was certainly hatchet-faced and, indeed, not far from axe-faced. The severe angles of his jaw, his cheekbones, and the sides of his forehead looked distinctly dangerous, Pontius thought, when he finally got a proper look at him. "Chiselled" would have been a more polite description. But, no: chiselled suggested a degree of good looks, and this man was far too angular to be called handsome. He had gathered a small crowd of islanders on the quay, anxious to see what he had for sale. Trading boats were so rare these days.

Pontius tried to push his way through with a selection of apologies:

'pardon me' ... 'make way, if you would be so kind' ... 'step aside sir, if you please.' None of these produced any result, except that he was told to wait his turn, like everyone else. It was left to Rissa to bellow, 'Clear the way. We are guardians,' before they could get through. Pontius imagined it was the voice she used to warn shipping off the rocks. It certainly produced a pathway through the crowd.

The hatchet-faced man broke into a grin.

'No need for a sea-going foghorn with *you* about, ma'am,' he observed.

The grin was even *more* hatchetty than his straight-faced expression.

Rissa glared at him.

'I am Rissa. Southern Guardian, Isle of Larus,' she said, and then added as an obvious afterthought, 'And this is the Reverend Pontius.'

'Eastern Guardian, Isle of Larus,' said Pontius since Rissa seemed disinclined to give him his full title.

The sea captain looked from one to the other, apparently unsure of which was the senior dignitary.

'We have four guardians on this isle,' said Rissa, looking down her nose. 'The other two are ... detained on important business elsewhere. You may deal with either of us. You wish to bring goods ashore to trade, yes?'

'I do, ma'am.'

'Very well, proceed,' said Rissa. 'I will leave the Reverend here to oversee the trading. I have important matters to attend to.'

Pontius opened his mouth to object to this unilateral decision, but she had already swept off in a swirl of scarlet skirts and was disappearing back up the hill.

'I do apologise, sir,' said Pontius. 'She is a little ... brusque. Please do proceed with the trading. Everyone is impatient to begin, I think.'

With a wave of their captain's hand, the crew began to unload boxes, crates, and baskets of goods. This was much to the delight of the people of Larus, who surged forward to get to the best bargains. Pontius and the sea-captain were good-naturedly shoved out of the way.

'Ooh, such manners!' said Pontius, brushing down his sleeves from the barging about. 'I apologise again, sir. Welcome to Larus.'

'We always call it "The Merry Isle", Reverend. And they do seem right merry, too,' said the sea-captain.

'Forgive me, I have not introduced myself. My name is Huxmix, master of the barque *Endeavour*. We called her that because she sails on forever ... and ever ... and ever,' he added, with a chuckle.

Pontius looked blank.

'Just my crew's little joke, sir,' said Master Huxmix, with another scary grin.

'Er, yes, Master Hixmux ...' Pontius was sure that wasn't right and stopped in confusion.

'Huxmix,' said the sea-captain, jovially. 'Not to worry, sir, everyone gets it wrong. Believe me, I have heard every possible version in my time, from Muxhox to Axemix.'

Not only a face like an axe, Pontius couldn't help thinking, but a name like one too.

'Do not concern yourself, Reverend, I answer to any of them!'

'Huxmix,' said Pontius, thinking it was a basic politeness to get a person's name right, even when the man himself had offered such tempting alternatives. 'Huxmix.'

'There, sir, you have it! Takes most people a week, and some never do get it straight. Very gentlemanly of you, I'm sure.'

While the crowd haggled and bought the ship's wares, Pontius took the opportunity to ask a few questions.

'I don't suppose you have any news from the wider world, do you, sir? Specifically, has there been a maritime calamity in recent weeks? A shipwreck, perhaps?'

'Why, no, Reverend,' said Master Huxmix. 'Wrecked ships are commonplace in the winter, as I'm sure you know. But in such fine weather, in general, and light airs as we have had so far this summer ... well, it wouldn't sink a cockleshell, to be sure. But I have been far away in the south, so I can't answer for what might have happened hereabouts.'

'No sea battles?' asked Pontius, wondering if it sounded a very stupid question.

'Why, none of them, neither,' said the sea captain, his hatchet-face cracking into an alarming smile.

'Not for many years, no. Whatever put such an odd idea into your head, Reverend, sir?'

Pontius was unwilling to say more. He knew the people wouldn't mention the presence of their merman. After all, if others learned about him, they might want one of their own and try to steal him. He would be jealously guarded, and the best guard was perfect silence.

'We receive little news of the wider world,' said Pontius, carefully, 'but I like to keep abreast of what goes on. Just idle curiosity, sir, no more. I suppose you wouldn't have, among your stock of items for sale, a shirt suitable for a man of the cloth, such as myself, would you?'

'I have just the very thing, Reverend,' said the sea-captain, with another hatchetty grin.

'Finest linen, and very reasonably priced. If you will just step this way ...'

The Reverend had been right: not a soul had said a word about their merman and, when the tide turned, the *Endeavour* sailed away in perfect, happy ignorance of there being any such thing on the merry Isle of Larus.

Spats in the Belfry

Even as he recovered, Captain Castello was strangely reluctant to venture out beyond the chapel. Pontius respected his need for solitude and kept the curious at arm's length, so the Captain wasn't bothered with visitors. During Sunday services, the door to the circular room under the belfry was kept firmly shut, to preserve Castello's privacy. There were many queries to answer regarding the health of their merman: were his gills troubling him? Had his tail regrown in a satisfactory way? Pontius bore this with fortitude, pointing out over and over again that the gentleman was not a merman, but a mortal with lungs and legs like everyone else. But the rumours persisted, and Pontius knew they would only be dispelled when Castello came out and walked about the Isle, for all to see.

'He isn't fully recovered, yet,' Pontius said, to answer the queries, whether kindly meant or purely curious.

'He will come out and meet you all soon enough.'

But Castello was reluctant.

'I have nothing but my name, Reverend,' he said sadly. 'I have nothing to tell them. I will be no more than an object of pity.'

To encourage him, Pontius brought him things to wear: a borrowed set of well-worn fishermen's clothing. Castello was persuaded to put them on, cutting a dishevelled and ragged figure. He begged a needle and thread and set to work, to alter and mend the clothes, but he still wouldn't leave the chapel.

He needs something to do, Pontius thought, something to take his mind off his lack of a past, his lack of memories—and perhaps create a few new ones. What could he suggest that might require his guest to venture outside the chapel a little? And then he had a brainwave. 'Would you like to look at my buckled bell?' he asked, one morning.

Castello's eyes lit up.

'Oh, indeed I would! How do I reach it?'

'Well,' said Pontius, pointing at the trapdoor above his room, 'it's up there. We'll need the ladder. I used to climb up there myself, in my younger days, but my knees ... you understand. No trouble for someone as spry as yourself, Captain, I'm sure.'

'What exactly is the problem, Reverend?' asked Castello, staring up at the ceiling.

'Ah. It was a ship's bell, you see. Rescued from a wreck, well before my time,' said Pontius. 'It suffered a battering in the sea. Frightful storm, they say. They used to have it on a wooden frame, for alarms. When they built the chapel for me, they set up a proper belfry while they were about it. But no one could get the dent out of it, and, in short my dear sir, it goes *clang* when it ought to go *bong*.'

'I see,' said Castello, who believed in his heart of hearts that there was nothing that couldn't be set to rights with careful polishing.

'Where d'ye keep the ladder, Reverend?'

Pontius was delighted at this enthusiastic response.

'It's tucked down the side of the aisle. Come, I'll show you.'

The bell was still used for alarms, of course, as well as chapel purposes. The occasional shipwreck had led to its untuneful tone being used to call the islanders out. But these were occasions Pontius could count on the fingers of one hand. On the whole, its clanging marked weddings, funerals, and Sunday morning services only.

While they carried the ladder in, Pontius continued the story of the chapel.

'Used to be two little cottages, you see ... fallen out of use ... no roof.'

He was puffing to keep up with Castello, who was ahead of him with the front of the ladder.

'They rebuilt it for me ... most kind ... and added the belfry ... with the round room underneath for me to live in ... and moved the bell up there ... you can see the rope goes through the hole in the trapdoor ... all very ingenious ... please mind the crockery with the end of the ladder, sir, I beg you.'

It was a near miss for the Reverend's milk jug in such a confined space, and he fussed about rescuing fragile objects as Castello set up the ladder.

The appalling noise was getting on the Reverend's nerves.

'I wish I had never mentioned it,' he muttered, as the bell gave another tuneless clang.

Castello had decided to attend to the bell *in situ*, rather than take it outside, as Pontius had hoped. And now, as he sat at the far end of the chapel trying to write a sermon, he sincerely wished the thing had never been brought out of the sea.

Castello was doing his best to muffle it, but his painstaking work announced itself at every move. The belfry had been designed to amplify the sound and was doing an excellent job.

People had been in and out all morning, asking if there was a shipwreck, or a pirate invasion, and Pontius was having his patience tried by all the interruptions.

'The bell is under repair,' he said, for the umpteenth time, 'please tell everyone there is no need for alarm. I hope it might be finished shortly.'

But when he asked Castello, asked him twice because he was now slightly deafened, he was told that yes, it would be finished shortly: no more than two or three days. Maybe four.

At this point, Pontius gave up and took his sermon-writing kit as far away as he could. But nowhere on the Isle of Larus was safe from the mournful, muffled clangs.

'Oh, I wish I'd never said a word about it,' he muttered with genuine feeling.

In the end, it went on for three interminable days, and Pontius was deeply thankful to see an end to it.

Castello was brimming with enthusiasm for his project, and keen to show off his handiwork.

'Ready, Reverend?' he asked. 'One ... two ... three—*go!*'

Pontius obediently gave the rope a firm, no-nonsense tug, steeling himself for the familiar clang. But no. The bell sang out with a fine, clear voice, reverberating tunefully round the Reverend and sending pleasing musical shivers into his very bones.

Captain Castello watched him anxiously, hoping for a happy reaction.

'My dear sir,' said Pontius, 'you have cast a magical spell upon it. You have taken it from a sad, flat clang to a sound positively ... orchestral!'

'Is that good?' asked Castello, still lacking confidence in his own abilities. 'Do you like it?'

'Like it?' said Pontius. 'Why, I am enraptured. Such a joy to the eardrums! I thank you very kindly for all your efforts, sir, on behalf of everyone on Larus.' He silently took back all the rude things he had privately said about Castello and the bell, while repairs were in progress.

'It is a marvel we shall all enjoy.'

Castello was visibly pleased at this reception and begged the Reverend to ring it again.

'I'll just go out and hear it from the outside, to be sure it's right,' he said and bustled out of the chapel.

Pontius pulled the rope.

'Bong,' said the bell.

'One for the Isle,' said a knowing voice in the Reverend's ear. But there was no one there. So, thought Pontius, that was indeed the first task.

The Ship of the Sky

It was only a small tree: a scrubby elder, bald on the windward side, and thinly leaved where there was a little shelter. It had insinuated its root under the corner of the building, more as an anchorage to stop it blowing away than anything else. Every year it grew a hopeful crop of leaves, and an even more hopeful flowerhead or two, though it never succeeded in setting fruit. The salt winds scorched it, blackening the foliage, and leaving the majority of the corky twigs bare most of the year. It wasn't much of a tree at all.

The bird didn't mind. It was somewhere to perch safely off the ground, and a song-post, too. So, there it was, singing away, minding its own business, when something quite large, quite hot, and making a rushing noise flew overhead. It skipped over a wall and landed with a crash in the distance. The bird just had time to be indignant, to wonder what sort of flying thing *that* might be having the audacity to interrupt its perfectly legitimate morning song, before the little shockwave arrived, a bit late. And, landing with a puzzled expression and its feet in the air, the bird fell out of the tree.

Cheerfully unaware of any kind of avian trauma, the Reverend Pontius had at last tempted Captain Castello out of the chapel.

'Just a little walk, sir. It is wonderfully beneficial to the digestion, you know. Fresh air, the very thing for good workings of the gizzards, according to my copy of *The Old Salte's Guide to the Worlde*. A very knowledgeable work on all matters; I heartily recommend it to you, sir.'

Castello, walking squinty-eyed after the gloom of the chapel, said he would certainly apply himself to reading it at the earliest opportunity.

A small girl ran laughing towards them, tripped over the hem of her overlong, hand-me-down petticoats, went sprawling, picked herself up, still laughing, and made an awkward curtsey.

'Goodness me,' said the Reverend Pontius, as she brushed herself down. 'It isn't ladylike to run like that, is it? Have you skinned your knees?'

'They's my knees,' said the child. 'Leave 'em be. Doesn't hurt.'

Pontius realised he was being told to mind his own business.

'So long as you've not hurt yourself,' he said.

'No,' said the child, and paused. She had clearly prepared a speech and the tripping up had confused her.

'Oh, yes. Mr Reverend, sir, there is a message from *that lady*. Gave me a sweet to come and tell you.'

"That lady", Pontius understood, was Mistress Rissa, the newly appointed southern guardian of the Isle. People said she was too young to take on such a responsibility, despite the best of qualifications. Pontius rather thought so himself, though he had in fact been younger than her when he had become eastern guardian. But that fact

rather slipped his mind. In any case, he had learned over time that it was better to keep his opinions to himself on such matters. He would simply be told that the Spirit of the Sea chose people to be guardians and that it was none of his business. Besides, the lady was perfectly able to fight her own battles.

'You mean Mistress Rissa,' he said, pointedly.

'Yes,' said the child, '*that lady.*'

'That is disrespectful,' Pontius persevered. 'She is not only our southern guardian, but also our ship-warden and wise woman of the weather.' People were beginning to refer to Rissa as "the lady ship-warden", so Pontius adopted that title for her, too. 'You may call her the lady "ship-warden", but not "that lady". Do you understand?'

The girl nodded. She had glazed over a little, while Pontius was speaking.

'Anyway, Reverend, sir, that lady ship-warden says you must come.'

'I am conducting Captain Castello on a brief walk for the good of his health. Tell her I will be along soon enough.'

The child stamped her foot. 'No, no, sir. She says you must come *now*.'

Pontius bristled. He wasn't on more than nodding terms with the lady ship-warden, not really. Getting to know her better was a long way down his things-to-do list, particularly since the arrival of Castello. Who was she to be ordering people about? From what he had heard, she was beginning to make a habit of it. Well, she wouldn't be ordering *him* about, thank you very much.

'I shall be along when I am ready,' he said firmly.

'What does she want me for, anyway?'

The child gave him a sly "that's-for-me-to-know" sort of look, and then thought better of it.

'Oh, sir,' she said, 'something has fallen out of the sky. She says you has the ear of the Spirit of the Sky, so you should see to it.'

Pontius began to bluster. He couldn't help himself.

'How dare she ...? What has fallen? Who is she to ...? What is it? Impossible woman! From the sky? No, I won't be ...' He trailed off, realising Castello was watching him closely. He was arguing with a small child, and, what's more, the child seemed to be winning. She stood her ground, smirking. Pontius caved in, as he usually did with the islanders.

'Very well, tell her I'll deal with it. She is at the Great Rock, is she?'

'Yes,' said the child, and began to skip away, and then stopped. 'But the thing that fell out of the sky is at Ferro the blacksmith's. That's where she says to go. Oh, and you had better take your merman with you.' She skipped away.

'He is *not* a merman,' called Pontius, faintly. 'And he certainly isn't mine!'

Castello gave him a sideways look. Pontius harrumphed, shook himself, and said, 'Come along then, Captain, our walk has a purpose now, though I'm sure it's all nonsense and there is nothing to see. It isn't far. I shall introduce you to our ship-warden and southern guardian at a later stage.'

'Charmed,' said Castello. 'I'm sure I shall be.'

I shouldn't depend upon it, Pontius thought. But he kept that notion to himself.

'Anything that falls out of the sky must be a gift from the Spirit of the Sky,' said the Reverend Pontius, dogmatically. 'Even if we don't know what it is.'

Whatever it was, people pointed out that it had fair put the wind up Mrs Ferro's best milking goat. Just look at her. The goat was in the corner of the paddock, pressed up against the stone wall, eyes wide, and still snorting with fright. Mrs Ferro herself was approaching purposefully, wearing a deep frown and a torn apron. 'We'll have nothing but ready-made cheese out of her for a week,' she said to Pontius, as if he could be expected to do something about it.

Pontius found himself on the brink of an apology, as if it actually were his fault, but pulled himself together in time. There was nothing to apologise for. The Spirit of the Sky had sent them a gift, and if part of that was a nervous goat producing ready-made cheese, then so be it.

People had gathered, and were staring at the object and the slightly smoking dent it had made in the paddock.

'Is it a star fallen out of the sky?' someone asked.

'Er ... well ...' Pontius had no idea. So he passed the question on.

'What do you think, Captain?'

Castello looked alarmed when all eyes turned on him. He had no idea either. If this truly were a fallen star, it was an odd-looking thing, and more than a little disappointing for something that was usually considered beautiful. He stroked his chin and made a guess.

'I don't believe that's a fallen star.'

Pontius rushed to offer support.

'I agree with the Captain. It isn't my idea of a star. Too much metal work, don't you think?'

'Aye,' said Castello, relieved, 'far too much metal work. Though it's strange metal, isn't it? What does the blacksmith say?'

'Where *is* Master Ferro?' asked Pontius, silently applauding Castello's excellent ploy of passing the question on to someone else.

Ferro the blacksmith was busy being torn off a strip by Mrs Ferro, for allowing such a thing to fall into the paddock and frighten the goat, so he was quite glad of an excuse to come and examine the object. He was reluctant to touch it, though.

'Whatever it is, it's broke,' he said, ignoring Pontius' roll of the eyes for stating the obvious.

'Looks burnt. No ironwork on it, but some of it's a sort of metal, for sure. These bits at the top ... a bit buckled, but they look like sails.'

Sails! Ferro was talking their language and people crowded closer, nodded wisely, and agreed. Very like sails.

'If they are sails, we can use them,' said Pontius, jumping on the bandwagon with unseemly haste.

'The Spirit will show us how. It is a wonderful gift.'

Mrs Ferro and her goat looked as if they might choose to disagree but were over-ruled.

Captain Castello looked again at the object and said, 'Sails, indeed. Reverend, I do believe this is a ship of the sky!'

A Different Degree of Oddness

'I had no idea Larus was such a dangerous place,' said Captain Castello, keeping a wary eye on the sky in general, and the bit above his head in particular, just in case anything else might suddenly fall out of it.

'Supposing that thing had fallen through somebody's roof? Supposing it had fallen through the chapel roof, Reverend?'

Pontius, who had also been casting a nervous eye or two skywards, which he hoped had gone unnoticed, said, 'We must trust in the Spirit of the Sky not to go hurling gifts through our roofs, Captain.'

He hoped he sounded confident.

'Especially not the chapel roof.'

Castello shrugged.

'I'm not sure Mrs Ferro's goat would share your optimism, sir. The Spirit's aim would seem to be less than perfectly accurate.'

'Mmm,' said Pontius, a little uncomfortable. He wasn't about to argue this point with a captain of artillery, so he changed the subject.

'I'm sure the people will find a good use for this "ship of the sky", as you call it.'

'I'm sure of it,' said Castello, 'something of benefit to us all.'

Us, thought Pontius; he said *us*, not *you*.

'I'm sure everyone will be grateful, sir, for such an, er, generous gift,' he said, but his mind had already moved on. The Spirit of the Sky *was* responsible for this new arrival, wasn't it? Not the Spirit of the Sea? It did have the hallmarks of the sea-spirit's playful nature, though. The Reverend resolved to ask the Spirit of the Sky for clarification in his prayers, just to make sure, though in a secret part of his soul, he knew he might just as well ask Mrs Ferro's goat.

If nothing else, the whole odd episode of the ship of the sky had brought Castello out into the community, taken him out of himself in a quite striking way. He talked animatedly about it, all the way back to the chapel. Pontius listened, nodded, agreed, and generally made encouraging noises.

'Tell me, Reverend, do odd things of this kind happen frequently here?'

Pontius looked carefully at Captain Castello to see if he were being serious. But even after a relatively short acquaintance, he knew the Captain wasn't much given to making jokes, and his open expression confirmed this. Quite in earnest.

'Well,' said Pontius, who had a limited sense of humour himself, and was thus inclined to be wary.

'I'd say no ... Or yes ... Perhaps ... Sometimes.'

Captain Castello found this answer perplexing, and he inclined his head to ask another question, but couldn't find the right one, so he raised an eyebrow instead. Pontius didn't yet know him well enough to judge whether this was a positive response or not, so he tried again.

'The thing is, my dear sir, odd things *have* happened over the years, but it's difficult to judge just how odd they are. Or even whether they're odd at all.' Castello still looked perplexed, so Pontius went on, 'From the days of my youth, I have no particular recollection of anything being odd. Scarcely anything.'

In fact, now that he thought about it, his life had been entirely ordinary and dull right up to the moment he had first heard of the Isle of Larus. Now that had been odd, hadn't it? The words had appeared on a to-do list in his own pocket, "Isle of Larus, enquire re" it had said. And he had been quite sure he hadn't written it himself, although the handwriting was undoubtedly his own. He opened his mouth to tell this to Castello and then stopped.

I cannot say that. He will think me quite crazed.

Instead, he stroked his chin, while he wondered what he *could* say.

'I believe ... well ... can I offer you a small measure of brandy?' This was blatant playing for time, but he hoped it might work.

'Most acceptable, most kind,' murmured Castello, who wasn't much of a drinker, but was far too polite to refuse such generous hospitality.

'Purely medicinal ...' said Pontius, 'do you good ... keeps out the cold.'

It was an uncomfortably warm day, but Castello said nothing, and they went into the chapel. Pontius clattered about with glasses, thinking furiously. There had been quite a number of odd things, both on his journey to Larus, and during his residence on the Isle. But was it safe to say so? The Larus people seemed to accept most things, however weird, with equanimity. Anything strange would be a nine-days'-wonder, and then quietly forgotten. The Reverend had learned that in general, it was best not to ask too many awkward questions. It just unsettled people, and if answers were not to be found, what was the purpose anyway? But Captain Castello was a logical man, and that was different. They settled down with their small measures of brandy (the stuff didn't grow on trees, now, did it?) and the Captain looked pointedly at Pontius, still awaiting an answer. Pontius hoped he wasn't expecting anything *too* logical.

'Well, as we were saying. Odd things ....' Pontius was desperate for something he could say on the subject without getting himself into deep water.

'I suppose ... we *could* say that your own arrival here, half-dead in a ship's boat, with no recollection of how you came to be there, was quite an odd event.'

Castello disagreed.

'Not really odd. Could happen to anyone.' He was on the defensive now.

'Forgive me, sir,' said Pontius, a little disgruntled, 'but I've never heard of it happening to anyone else.'

'I'll grant you it's *unusual*,' said Castello, 'but not *impossible*. I expect there was an accident ...' He stared out of the chapel window for a while, lost in thought.

'But it's not odd in the way that a ship, with sails, falling out of the sky is odd. Not the same *degree* of oddness at all.'

Pontius had to concede.

'Not the same degree of oddness, you are right. A strange thing will wash up on the beach from time to time, something that is ... difficult to identify. On Larus, they either bury it, burn it, or find a use for it, whatever it might have been to begin with. Half the houses on the island have peculiar objects built into their fabric. Some of them are bits of wrecked ships, but not all. If the people have a practical use for it, they stop asking questions. I've no doubt they will find a use for your ship of the sky, or some of it, anyway.'

'Are any of these "*peculiar objects*" built into the chapel, Reverend?' asked Castello. 'I should be interested to see them.'

'As a matter of fact, they are. And you shall see them,' said Pontius, brightly. He congratulated himself for dodging the question so neatly and finding something to take the Captain's mind off it, too. I'll tell him more when the time is right, Pontius thought. *Or perhaps I won't.*

The Scarlet Woman

As Castello's health improved, and his confidence slowly grew, the Reverend Pontius decided it was time to formally introduce him to the other three guardians. It wasn't something he specially looked forward to, since, in all honesty, he was only really on nodding terms with them himself. He decided to begin with the southern guardian, Rissa. She was the toughest one to deal with, and they might as well get that over with first.

'I have to warn you, sir, the lady is a little ... er ... irascible.'

Pontius picked his words carefully as they headed to the southern tip of the island, in case they might be repeated later. Should he have said "irascible"? Was he absolutely sure of its meaning? Would anybody else know? A word of at least nine letters was generally a pretty safe bet, he had found. Still, if the lady herself should hear it, would she mind? It was too late to worry about it now, Pontius thought. It had been said, and that was that, but only to Captain Castello. The Captain himself frowned.

'Irascible, Reverend?'

Oh, dear. 'Well, I mean to say, a little temperamental.' No, that wouldn't do either. 'Sensitive.' Surely no woman would object to that. But "sensitive" wasn't the half of it; Rissa, the ship-warden and southern guardian of Larus, was notoriously tetchy. Yes, that was the word, but Pontius wasn't about to use it. Nor would he admit he was terrified of her. The best way to deal with her, as far as the Reverend was concerned, was to avoid her at all costs. But in this instance, he couldn't. Introductions had to made, or she might feel slighted.

'I beg you, have a care of her sensibilities, Captain. She is easily offended, you see.'

This was putting it very mildly indeed. Rissa could take offence at practically *anything*, and her rages lasted for *ages*.

'I shall be the very soul of discretion,' said Castello.

You'd better be, thought Pontius, or she'll box your ears for you. He said no more. There was nothing to be gained by getting their acquaintance off to a bad start before it had even begun. *Who knows? They may even like one another.* Pontius struggled to imagine anyone actually *liking* the lady ship-warden, but then, interpersonal relationships always rather baffled him. He could only trust that two such formally minded individuals could meet without a quarrel developing. Goodness knows, Pontius thought, she has quarrelled with just about everyone else. It never occurred to him that her position as the only female guardian on Larus might be responsible for her sensitivity to criticism.

'Mistress Rissa, may I present Captain Castello,' said Pontius, as they stood before her. She was, as always, dressed entirely in red, a uniform of sorts, so she stood out like a beacon to ships venturing too close to the island's rugged coastline. The Reverend was used to it, but Castello was boggle-eyed. There will be no need for flourishes, Pontius thought, she won't appreciate them. The less said the better: a simple pleasantry or two, and we'll be on our way, duty satisfied.

But to his dismay Castello produced a few flourishes all on his own.

'Your servant,' he said, and made an unnecessarily courtly bow. 'I have heard so much about you, Mistress Rissa.'

No, thought Pontius, no, please do not continue. But it was too late.

Rissa had raised an eyebrow at the bow, inclined her head in return, and was already saying,

'Oh? And what have you heard?'

Castello realised that what he had heard were words like "irascible" and "temperamental". He floundered. 'Ah, that is to say …'

Pontius came to his rescue.

'I was just telling the Captain how much you are esteemed on the Isle, of your great work as southern guardian and ship-warden, of the excellent way in which you preserve the safety of Larus and its fishing fleet.'

He paused, sure he had forgotten something. 'Oh, and as wise woman of the weather, too. Of course.'

Rissa seemed mollified, and Pontius breathed again. *That was a near-run thing.* All they had to do was apologise for taking up so much of her valuable time and move on. But there was Castello, opening his mouth to speak again. Pontius made desperate, small, shaking movements of his head. Castello didn't see them, but Rissa did, and she glared at Pontius.

'Such great responsibilities you bear, ma'am,' Castello said, 'for a ...'

Oh dear. Pontius took a step backwards; the lady ship-warden had been known to hurl missiles when she was upset.

'For a what?' she asked. 'For a woman?'

If Pontius had been able to retreat to a safe and private place, where he could sit with his head in his hands, he would have done so.

'Oh,' he said, 'I'm sure the Captain didn't mean ...'

But Castello hadn't finished being courtly. It usually worked with women, after all.

'For such a refined and elegant lady as yourself,' he said, with another exaggerated bow.

Rissa shook out her scarlet skirts, making Pontius cringe.

'The tempest does not blow any the less violently upon me, sir, refined and elegant or not. The great waves will sweep me off my feet and hurl me to perdition just as readily as they will you. The weather recognises no difference: man or woman. Or lady. No ship was ever spared the rocks of Larus because it carried female passengers. I learned the weather lore at my father's feet, sir, and I am blessed with exceptional eyesight for ship-watching. I have *earned* my place as southern guardian.'

'Oh,' said Castello, 'no ... I'm sure ... very competent ... most able ...'

Pontius took another wary step back. The situation was beyond help. Rissa was just getting into her stride.

'And what would you know about it, sir? Sea captain, are you?'

'Captain of artillery,' said Castello, defensively.

'Ah, artillery!' said Rissa. 'And that would qualify you to judge my ship-watching and weather-forecasting efficiency, would it?'

Too late, thought Pontius, to run for shelter. A vicious squall was already upon them.

'Bah!' she said and turned away just long enough for Pontius to swiftly grasp Castello by the arm, in an effort to remove him from her line of fire. But not swiftly enough. Rissa had reached into a capacious pocket in her skirts and extracted a large handful of bladderwrack.

'Perhaps you'd like to try your hand at weather forecasting, sir.'

She threw the seaweed with a force that caught Castello by surprise. And the seaweed caught him full in the face. He had to admit, she was an excellent shot.

'Just the thing for a *merman*, I believe,' she said, and stalked off in a swish of scarlet.

Castello brushed the seaweed away absent-mindedly.

'What a woman!' he murmured.

Pontius couldn't tell if the Captain were impressed or horrified. Pontius, himself, was definitely horrified.

'Come,' he said, attempting to sound as if nothing had happened, 'we shall continue our tour of the Isle, shall we?'

'Mmm,' said Castello, still watching the retreating Rissa.

Ye gods, thought Pontius, he is smitten.

They had walked on for only a few minutes, when they were accosted by a small girl, quite breathless.

'Reverend. Sir. And Mr Merman. If you please,' she gasped. 'The lady ... the lady says to Mr Merman, she regrets ... regrets throwing the seaweed.'

Castello smiled and made a bow to the child. But she hadn't finished.

'Regrets the seaweed ... and could she have it back? It is her best forecasting seaweed, you see.'

Pontius snorted. The cheek of it! And, besides, the seaweed was surely still on the ground, where it had fallen, wasn't it?

Castello hesitated a moment, blushed, and extracted the weed from his pocket. He handed the stuff over to the child and said, 'Please convey this to the lady, with my apologies. I hadn't realised it was valuable to her.'

The child ran off, leaving Pontius with his mouth open. Castello had pocketed that bit of smelly seaweed as a sort of keepsake. He had done it secretly, too. But not so secretly that Rissa hadn't noticed. I am sadly out of my depth, so far as dealings between men and women are concerned, Pontius thought. It is a serious failing, and one I should address without delay.

But at least he didn't need to take that into consideration before taking Castello to meet their western guardian, Rufus the Hermit.

The Sea Whisperer

The old man sat on a rock, staring west over the sea with empty eye-sockets, holding a long staff in one hand.

'Ah,' he said, at their approach, shifting on his uncomfortable-looking rock, 'it is you, Reverend. And our new guardian, too. Good day to you.'

'He lives in the past, I fear,' murmured the Reverend Pontius.

'It is many years since he was appointed as guardian.'

'Nonsense,' said Rufus the Hermit. 'I know where I am and when I am, thank you very much. I know what I'm talking about.'

He might be blind, but there was clearly nothing wrong with his hearing. Pontius ignored this remark and continued as he had intended.

'May I present to you Captain Castello? He is our guest on Larus.'

Castello was halfway through one of his courtly bows, when he realised it was pointless in front of a blind man.

'Your servant, sir,' he said, straightening up.

'Ah, yes,' said Rufus, smiling now. 'I have heard all about *you*. You are our merman, are you not?'

Pontius rolled his eyes.

'He is not a merman. It is a foolish rumour.'

'Hmm,' said Rufus, still smiling. 'Yes. But the Spirit of the Sea has much to say about him.'

Pontius rolled his eyes again.

'He imagines he converses with the Spirit of the Sea,' he said, behind his hand, to Castello.

Rufus brought the foot of the staff down onto the rock with a crack, making them both jump.

'Do not patronise me, if you please, Reverend. Have a little respect for your seniors.'

Pontius rolled his eyes so far this time he was afraid they might roll clear out of his head.

'No offence intended, Colleague, I'm sure.'

'Hmm,' said Rufus. 'Well, what do you have to say for yourself, young man?'

Castello had been listening to this bat-and-ball conversation with his mouth slightly ajar and was caught unprepared for the question.

'Ah, hmm,' he said. 'Well ... Very honoured ... naturally ... delighted to make your ... very humble in the presence of ...'

'If you're going to talk rubbish, you may as well clear off,' said Rufus the Hermit with a shrug, throwing Castello into greater confusion.

'Oh! All possible apologies ... I did not intend ...' He looked in desperation at Pontius, who came to his rescue.

'What we would both like to know, Colleague, is what exactly the Spirit of the Sea had to say about Captain Castello.'

Castello nodded eagerly. He had got himself into such a hopeless tangle of compliments and apologies that it hadn't occurred to him to ask the obvious question.

'My conversations with the spirit are private,' said Rufus. 'Not for sharing with the hoi-polloi.'

This was beyond mere eye-rolling, and Pontius actually felt himself stamp his foot in frustration. '*Hoi-polloi?*'

'Temper, temper, Reverend,' said Rufus, with an inscrutable smile.

'What I *can* tell you is that a range of pressing problems will be presenting themselves, and that this gentleman, Castello, will have a hand in addressing them. That's all.' With that, he turned away from them and resumed staring sightlessly at the sea.

'Thank you for that ... um ... very remarkable *insight*, sir.' Pontius sneered.

'We will not interrupt your important sea-staring a moment longer. Good day.'

Castello had never heard Pontius speak so sarcastically to anyone. He was a little short-tempered at times, perhaps, but never spoke with such obvious rudeness. He was shocked. 'Good day to you, sir,' he said, with another pointless bow.

His shocked expression wasn't lost on Pontius.

'I apologise for that,' the Reverend said, as they walked back along the cliff path. 'But he tries my patience to the utmost with his airy-fairy nonsense.'

'I believe you should offer your apologies to Master Rufus, sir,' said Castello quietly, 'not to me.'

Pontius stared at the ground, ashamed and unable to answer.

It took Pontius a while to regain his composure, and they had left the cliff path before either of them spoke again.

'What do you think he meant?' Castello asked, at last, 'about the "pressing problems"?'

Pontius shook his head.

'Who knows, my dear sir? I have suffered these ridiculous predictions all these years. Master Rufus was a guardian here already, when I arrived, you see, and they are so very vague, they could apply to anything. A torn sail on a boat is a pressing problem to a fisherman, after all. Could you patch a sail, sir?'

'I believe I could,' said Castello, 'And I should be happy to help.'

'Well, there you are,' said Pontius.

'It may be as straightforward as that.' Except, he rather doubted it. He hoped he was wrong, but he felt in his bones that something rather odder than a torn sail was in the offing. However, he was certainly not about to worry Castello by saying so.

'Pinch of salt,' he said, 'we should take these things with a pinch of salt.'

Master Delphinus

'Well,' said Pontius, as they strode downhill together, 'I shall take you to meet our northern guardian, Master Delphinus. He is a little decrepit, I'm afraid, and wandering somewhat in his wits, these days. But he is a capital fellow, for all that. Lives with his daughter, down by the quay.'

Castello made no comment. He seemed a little wary, and still distracted by his encounter with Rissa the shipwarden. Pontius stole a sideways glance at his face. Poor fellow, he thought, knows not whether he's a-coming or a-going, as they say in these parts. He wasn't sure whether the Captain's being smitten with Rissa was a good thing or not.

On the one hand, it might help to keep him here on Larus. But on the other hand, if it went awry, which it very well might, given the lady's disdainful attitude, it might just as easily drive him away.

'Master Delphinus was a great stargazer, in his day,' Pontius observed, continuing the conversation single-handed, 'Oh, yes, and he named many stars—one of them after me. It is the forty-seventh star on the right and is Pontius Major. Master Delphinus always promised he would find another, to be Pontius Minor, but I fear he never quite got round to it.'

'Indeed,' said Castello eventually, clearly not paying full attention.

'Major and minor. Yes.'

Pontius huffed. It wasn't every day he had the opportunity to boast of having his very own star. Everyone on the island was aware of it, and it wasn't the kind of thing you dropped easily into casual conversation with the occasional passing boat crew. By the way, sir, I have my own star; did you know? That wouldn't do at all. But Castello, evidently an educated person, should have appreciated it, and his distracted reply was annoying.

'He also named one after Mrs Ferro's goat: Capra Temperamentalis,' said Pontius, just to see if Castello was actually listening.

'Temperamentalis,' said Castello, with another faraway look.

With a rare flash of insight, Pontius knew for certain that his friend could only be thinking of Rissa the ship-warden.

'Hmm. Temperamentalis, indeed,' he muttered.

The visit to Master Delphinus was brief. As Pontius had observed, the old fellow might be found to be reliably at home in person, but not always as far as his wits were concerned.

'You have just missed him, Reverend,' said the old man's daughter, fondly. 'He were here, all wits collected, just a little while since, and talking perfect sense. But now ... well ... as you see ...'

Master Delphinus sat, his huge dark eyes in a shrivelled face, staring at the ceiling, and acknowledging his visitors not at all.

'Pity,' said Pontius, shaking his head. 'He's quite engaging when he's at home. Fount of knowledge on all things astronomical, y'know. Very learned.' He leaned in close and said to the old man, 'Good day to you, sir. It is I, Pontius Major, and Minor to be, one day too, I trust.'

'Forty-seventh to the right,' said the old man, without taking his eyes off the ceiling. 'But no Minor, not yet.'

'See?' said Pontius. 'Very learned. But I don't think we shall have any conversation with him, not to speak of. What do you think, Mistress Petronilla?'

The daughter shook her head.

'He knows you are here, Reverend; he knows you by your star. But it's too much for him to say more.'

'Poor fellow,' said Castello, as they left the house. 'I should have liked to talk to him. Such a pity to let knowledge wither away, unshared.'

Pontius nodded, waiting for Castello to make the obvious comment, but it was a while before he stopped and said, 'How can Master Delphinus fulfil his role as northern guardian, given his ... indisposition?'

'To tell the truth, sir,' said Pontius, 'he never did, not really. His learned stargazing endeared him to the people. Some of the fishermen use the stars for navigation if they go out at night, though mostly they don't, and they don't stray far from the Isle. They appreciate a little learning here, even if they don't have much use for it.'

'Up and down this hill I go,' grumbled the Reverend Pontius, as he walked. 'I swear my legs are shorter every year, from the wear and tear.'

An urgent message had arrived from Mistress Petronilla. 'Urgent,' said Pontius to himself, 'they're *always* urgent.' It was true. He had never yet received one that said not to worry, no haste needed.

'I expect Master Delphinus has wandered off again. But why she thinks I will be any better at finding him than anyone else, I don't know.'

Still, it *could* be urgent. Master Delphinus, in his dotage, was inclined to wander in both mind and body, and there was always the worry that he might fall down a hole or walk into the sea in his confusion. His daughter, Petronilla, called on the whole island to help when her father went missing, and so far, he had been found, safe and sound each time, though in increasingly odd places.

'How long has he been gone?' barked Pontius, when Petronilla came out to meet him.

'Gone?'

'Yes, gone. When did you last see him?'

'Why, not two minutes since, Reverend. He is indoors.'

Pontius stared at her.

'So what is so very urgent? Is he ill again?'

'No, Reverend. He is as well as he ever is, these days. He has written a book, you see.'

Pontius didn't see at all. The pair of them seemed to be holding completely different conversations. He thought it best to begin again.

'Mistress Petronilla, why have you called me down?' He didn't add, *in the middle of my weekly pew-polishing duties, too, most inconvenient.*

Petronilla folded her hands in a gesture of great modesty and said, 'He has written a great book, Reverend, as I said. Very lengthy. He is insisting that it be published for the benefit of the world, and he has charged me with seeing to it. I have no notion at all how to do it, Reverend, so I am asking you to help me, as you are the most learned person in all the Isle, besides my father.'

That was quite well-put, Pontius thought, but he felt a painful stab in the heart. The old man had written a book! *And I have written nothing, though I often intended it.* There was that stab to the vitals again. Was it regret, or jealousy?

'It is his life's work,' Petronilla went on, unaware of any stabs to Pontius' vitals.

'His astronomical observations and conclusions. He says it is a great addition to the sum of knowledge, Reverend.'

'No doubt,' said Pontius, 'most scholarly, I'm sure. Tell me, have you read this work yourself, Mistress?'

'I have tried, sir. You taught me my letters yourself, of course, and I read and write moderate-well. But, in truth, my father's work is beyond me. I cannot make head nor tail of it, Reverend, which is why I am asking for your assistance. Would you look at it for me?' She moved closer and lowered her voice.

'My fear, sir, is that it is all nonsense. Not so much the observations: they are years old, most of them, and made when he was fully in his wits. It is the conclusions that worry me. They are recent-written, and he may not have been in his wits when he wrote them, if you get my drift, sir. Even if you *can* advise me on publication, I would not do it, if it shows my father a fool. I would not expose him to derision.'

'Ah.' Pontius understood perfectly.

'I see the difficulty. I am no hand at the astronomicals, but perhaps you would allow me to look at the book.'

'Yes, sir, of course.' Petronilla's tight and worried expression softened. She was a pleasant-looking woman when she smiled, Pontius couldn't help thinking.

'May I take it with me?' he asked. 'I'd like to study it properly.'

Petronilla beamed at this.

'I'll fetch it directly, Reverend, if you'll just wait a moment. I cannot ask you in, or my father may ask why you're here. What should I tell him if he asks where the book is?'

'Tell him it's gone to print,' said Pontius. 'His notion of time is a little hazy, is it not? It will satisfy him, I think.'

'Oh,' said Mistress Petronilla, 'I shall certainly tell him *that*. He will be delighted.'

And before Pontius could prevent it, she had called her father out and told him the Reverend was taking the book to be printed and wasn't that kind of him.

'Printed!' said Master Delphinus, almost skipping with excitement. 'Printed, indeed! It is my dearest wish. I am the happiest man alive.'

The Suit of Yellow

Later, Pontius sat with Master Delphinus' great work of literature and science before him, and his head in his hands. There were many, many, scribbled pages of tiny, cramped writing, scruffy calculations in the margins, rough sketches of constellations, and complex, fold-out maps of the heavens. It was all Greek to the Reverend Pontius.

The whole thing was set between two waterworn pieces of driftwood, playing the part of covers. It had been tied together with threadbare ribbon, no doubt formerly the property of Mistress Petronilla. It did resemble a real book, in a ramshackle sort of way.

Pontius scratched his head over it. When Castello came in, after a stint earning his keep by keeping the graveyard tidy, Pontius called him over.

'I can't make head nor tail of it,' he said, 'no more than Mistress Petronilla could. Do you know anything of astronomy, Captain?'

Castello had found that he never knew anything about anything until he tried, so he leafed through the pages.

'I believe,' he said at last, 'that it is as you and she feared, Reverend. The observations seem sound enough, but the conclusions are mostly gibberish.'

'I suppose we cannot correct them for him?' asked Pontius, without much hope of a positive reply.

Castello shook his head.

'It seems I know a little of the subject, but neither of us has the knowledge to set this to rights.'

'Oh,' said Pontius, making a resolution to never again offer to read anyone's book for them. 'Whatever am I to tell them? Even if we could arrange the printing, it would make him a laughingstock, and we cannot allow that. Master Delphinus thinks it has gone to be printed. I wish I hadn't said that. He will be so disappointed. What can we do?'

'As to that,' said Castello, thoughtfully, 'I have an idea.'

'But he will expect far more than we can possibly deliver,' said Pontius, wringing his hands. 'It is a very long book, a very weighty book—and half of it gibberish.'

Castello leafed through the manuscript again. It had clearly been a giant undertaking on the part of Master Delphinus: his life's work. 'Not quite gibberish, exactly, Reverend,' he said, 'but it is certainly very ... dense.'

'Not as dense as I am for making such rash promises about it,' said Pontius, in despair.

'Will I never learn to keep my mouth shut?' Captain Castello thought it unlikely and smiled secretly.

'But see here, Reverend, there are goats on the island, are there not?'

'Goats?' said Pontius, thrown by the sudden change of subject.

'Goats, my dear sir? What do *goats* have to do with it?'

'Well, Reverend, where there are goats, there will be goatskins. Do you think we could get hold of one?'

Pontius wrinkled his nose at the memory of the last time they had treated a goatskin.

'What did you have in mind?' he asked warily.

'Find me a goatskin and a pair of proper, flat boards, and I think I could bind this manuscript; at least well enough to please Master Delphinus. His eyesight is poor, and his memory is short. Might he not be persuaded to believe it is a *published* version of his book? It is a deception, I know, and you, as a man of the cloth could not be party to such a thing. But I could. It's a kindly meant deception, after all. What d'ye think?'

'I think you are a genius, sir,' said Pontius. 'And I think he will be very pleased with it. It is a very minor deception, in a very good cause, and I'm sure the spirit will overlook it. Just promise me you won't be tanning goatskins in the chapel, and I shall be a very happy man.'

It was, once again, a while before Pontius realised another task had been set. Had it been set by Mistress Petronilla, Master Delphinus, or

Castello himself? And did it much matter? The Reverend shrugged. *One for a friend.* Would that friend be Master Delphinus? Or might it refer to Pontius, as a friend of Castello? He rather hoped the latter might be the case.

It was no use pretending that the finished book was printed. Anyone with a serviceable pair of eyes could see that it was nothing of the sort. The question was, what would Master Delphinus make of it?

'His eyes are very dim,' said Pontius. 'He has spent so very much of his life peering through a telescope that his sight is perpetually focussed on the heavens. You can tell by the deterioration of his handwriting.'

'Hmm,' said Castello.

'The book is all quite logical at the beginning, but by the end he has half the pages partially written the wrong way up and sometimes sideways. And that's without considering the equations in the margins. They are at every possible angle.'

This untidiness had been a trial to Castello, who was happiest when things were well-ordered. He had done his best to make sense of it. The binding was as good as he could make it, but the actual written words bothered him.

'Some of the pages were odd sizes, too,' he fretted.

'I know, I know, my dear sir,' said Pontius. 'You have done wonders with it, considering. Wonders, I say. Order out of chaos, sir, no doubt about it. And the binding is a thing of beauty, given that you had nothing but a goatskin to work with.' He made a mental note to ask Castello how he made the skin, which had stunk to the very heavens when they acquired it, smell so sweet.

'If Master Delphinus rejects it, he is nothing but a nit-picking old fool ...'

Pontius paused. Whatever was he saying? Castello was staring with his mouth open. This was no way for a man of the cloth to be speaking.

'Um, what I mean to say is that I promised him a proper printed book. I should never have said it. My own fault entirely. And this is not a proper printed book, despite your excellent work, Captain.'

Castello smiled.

'Don't concern yourself, Reverend. If he questions it, we will tell him it is a *facsimile* copy, that it was far too good to entrust to an editor. That it remains exactly as he created it that he will not be able to tell it from the original, even down to the odd-sized pages.'

'Sir,' said Pontius, not for the first time, 'I salute you. You are a genius.'

'It's a little, er, hectic,' said the Reverend Pontius. 'Doesn't he mind it?'

Master Delphinus lit up the gloomy interior of the cottage, all on his own.

'It was a shade of green to begin with,' said his daughter, 'but then I washed it, and well, the colours ran, you see. The water turned blue, and my father's outfit was left yellow. But his eyes are so bad these days, Reverend, he says he sees it as a soft tan colour. Doesn't mind it at all. Thinks it quite elegant. And don't you dare tell him the true nature of it, either. He's happy as he is.'

'Wouldn't dream of it, ma'am,' said Pontius, 'not if he's happy.' He resisted the urge to shade his eyes from the sunny glare of Master Delphinus' suitings.

'Very stylish, I'm sure,' he said to Master Delphinus himself, who had shuffled over to the cottage door.

'What's that?'

'Ears are none too good, neither,' said Mistress Petronilla, fussing round her father. 'Comes to us all, Reverend.'

'Indeed,' said Pontius, averting his eyes as the exterior light caught the astronomer's outfit, so he glowed golden like a true star in their midst.

The Reverend Pontius had prepared a formal speech of presentation, but the sight of the old man in his glowing yellow clothing put the whole thing out of his head.

'My dear sir,' he waffled, 'esteemed colleague ... on behalf of ... um...er... delighted ... I'm sure ...'

'Yes, yes,' said Master Delphinus, smiling. 'I have no idea what you are talking about, sir, nor indeed who you might be, but I beg you to get on with it. There is a partial eclipse imminent, you know.'

'Oh,' said Pontius, a little deflated. 'Well, here it is. Your book, sir, with our best wishes.'

'Book?' said Master Delphinus, 'what book?'

'Why, *your* book, sir. Your life's work. Your astronomical observations. Look, we have bound it for you.'

'Very fine,' said Master Delphinus, squinting, 'oh, very fine. Who did you say had written it?'

'You yourself, sir,' said Pontius, feeling he was tumbling down a bottomless well of confusion. It was clear that he and Castello had been fretting about nothing.

'It is *your* book, your great work.'

'Is it so?' asked Master Delphinus, running his fingers over the binding. 'Must have slipped my mind. Very fine work.' He tried to hand it back to Pontius.

'No, no. It is for *you*, sir. To keep.'

The old man seemed to understand at last.

'I shall treasure it,' he murmured, and clung to it as if he would never let it go.

And, according to Mistress Petronilla, he never did; he slept with it under his pillow, as if he might reabsorb each night the mighty weight of knowledge he had now mostly forgotten.

Bell, Book, and Cannon

The book, though, did weigh on the mind of the Reverend Pontius in the succeeding days. It was clearly the second task. *One for a friend*. Was the friend in question Pontius himself—Castello had rescued him from a considerable predicament—or Master Delphinus? The Reverend thought it didn't matter much. Books, he thought idly. Oh, *books*! How long had it been, he wondered, since he had last spent a day in a library? He had quite lost count of the years. It had been such a natural part of life in his student days, reading under the eagle eye of the librarian. The fusty smell of treasured old books came back to him immediately. Such a reassuring odour, he thought, the scent of certainty and thoughtfulness.

Pontius moved directly to his own tiny library: just a few books on a wobbly shelf. He took one down at random and buried his face in its pages, inhaling deeply. *Aah!*

The book was *The Old Salte's Guide to the Worlde*; a volume of mainly seagoing wisdom, since that was the world the *Old Salte* clearly knew. It was the only new one Pontius had acquired in all his years on Larus. The people of the Isle had clubbed together and found enough things to barter it from a passing trading ship as a special gift for their eastern guardian. Well, the Reverend was a learned man, wasn't he? A man of letters who would surely appreciate any sort of book. The gift reflected the fact that he had patiently taught many of them to read and write.

It was the best gift Pontius had ever received, and he looked at it fondly. Inside the front cover was the unsteady inscription, "To the Revrende being from the poeple of Larus. With thanks."

Pontius smiled at the memory and looked with affection at the battered book; it carried the thumb marks of many a reader besides himself. He had spent many evenings straining his eyesight, lost in its pages and learning some very odd facts on seagoing matters. The *Old Salte*, Pontius had noted, was something of an unreliable narrator, with many self-contradictions appearing on the book's pages. But never mind; he loved it anyway, and often quoted its questionable wisdom in the hope of sounding like less of a landlubber. The Larus fishermen indulged him when he attempted to lecture them on the correct tying of knots or give them handy hints on boat repair.

'I do wonder what became of the rest of my books,' Pontius said aloud, not for the first time, though he had long since conceded he would probably never know the answer. He had come to Larus so long ago now, bearing only what he could carry and only three of his books had made it into the bundle. The rest had been left with his old mentor, Father Ormerod. Pontius had written, soon after his arrival on the Isle, to request they be sent on to him. But who could say whether the letter (and the money contained in it) had ever been received? Had some sailor weighed the package, heard the jingle of coins, and broken into it? Had the coins been pocketed, and the precious message thrown carelessly overboard? Or had Father Ormerod received it and refused to send the books out of sheer spite? They had not parted on good terms, after all. Pontius didn't know the letter's fate.

He thought of sending again, to enquire. But was Father Ormerod still living? It was a long time ago, and the likelihood, Pontius knew, was that his books had long since been donated to the college library. He hoped they might do some good there.

He looked sadly at his own pitiful library, and an idea began to form. If Master Delphinus could write a book of his own, then why couldn't he? Something a little more reliable than *The Old Salte's Guide*, though. Now, there was an interesting thought.

'I shall need a new shelf for all the volumes,' he said to himself, indulging in a daydream of himself as a respected author, 'maybe even two.'

He was just reaching the point of needing three shelves, and wondering whether the construction of them might constitute another task for Captain Castello, when the man himself came through the chapel door.

'Bookshelves,' said Pontius, still in a literary daze.

Castello stared at him.

'Yes indeed, Reverend. Might I have a word? If you don't find yourself too busy?'

'I may need three,' said Pontius, still thinking libraries, 'for all the volumes, you see.'

'I'm sure you shall,' said Castello. 'But I need to speak with you, Reverend. Will you walk with me? It is a very fine day outdoors.'

Pontius understood at last that Castello had something on his mind that related not at all to books. He fetched his coat and hat, and they set out along the top of the Isle.

They walked a good distance in silence, Castello obviously struggling with what he had to say. Pontius had the good sense not to prompt him, but let him begin in his own good time. As they came to the northern end of the island, the splendid view of harbour and quayside opened up before them, step by step. But neither of them was really paying attention to it, the Captain distracted and Pontius still with half his mind on the shelves loaded with his learned writings.

'It has been a fine holiday I have had,' said Castello, suddenly rather formal, 'but I am quite recovered now, and I feel I have imposed upon you long enough.'

'What?' said the Reverend Pontius, stopping in his tracks.

'I ... oh, my dear sir ... there is no need ...'

Castello silenced him with a raised hand.

'Long enough,' he said.

Pontius felt his jaw fall open, and the rest of him fall into turmoil. Did the Captain really think he had outstayed his welcome? Surely he must know that he had not. Or was he just testing the water, being polite? Pontius spluttered, 'No need at all ... most welcome ...'

There was no denying the accommodations at the chapel were a little cramped with two occupants, but Pontius had *so* enjoyed the company—having someone to talk to. He had barely forced his jaw back up into a suitably closed position before an even worse thought struck him. *Is it me he wishes to escape from? Is it my eternal prattling that drives him away? Does he dislike me?* Down went the Reverend's jaw again.

Castello, who rarely observed a gesture in *anyone* without completely misinterpreting it, understood that Pontius had been waiting with increasing impatience to see the back of him.

Pontius himself, meanwhile, had regained control of his wayward jaw and managed to say, 'But where would you go, my dear sir?' He dreaded the answer. Would Castello leave not only the chapel, but the island? For the first time in his adult life, Pontius felt he had found a friend and the thought of losing that friendship made his lower lip threaten to wobble.

'I shall take lodgings,' said Castello, evenly, 'and await the next boat to the mainland.'

Poor Pontius. His worst fears were realised. Down went his jaw again, he simply couldn't help it. *How can I keep him, my only real friend, here on Larus?* Surely it was sinful to try to restrict the freedom of another. Wasn't it? Was it a sinful action even to wish Castello might stay? Pontius rolled his eyes skyward in a silent plea to the Spirit of the Sky for clarification, or better still, practical assistance.

Castello, observing this, misunderstood again and said, 'I shall be out of your way as soon as it can be arranged, Reverend, and I thank you sincerely for all your care these last weeks.'

Pontius, still struggling to keep his face under control, stared downhill towards the harbour while he tried to frame a reply that wouldn't make matters worse. Something on the harbour edge caught his eye, something dully glinting in the sun. The Reverend's jaw snapped shut, and then arranged itself into a small smile. Why had he not thought of this before?

'Let us not fret about all that just now, Captain. What do you say we walk down and inspect the cannon at the old castle, eh?'

'Oh,' said Castello, brightening. He could never resist a piece of artillery, however neglected. 'Oh, I should like that very much.'

'Come along then,' said Pontius and, as they walked purposefully downhill, he secretly rolled his eyes skywards and mouthed, 'Thank you. *One for himself*, I think.'

Captain Castello's eyes filled with tears.

'Oh, my dear sir,' said Pontius, taken by surprise, 'I am so sorry. I did not intend to ... I thought you might like ... that is to say ...' He trailed off, unsure of what he could do to set things right. This had been a sad mistake.

'Oh, no,' said Castello, sniffing manfully.

'No, I assure you, Reverend, it is just the condition of them that distresses me.' He threw his arms affectionately around a cannon's barnacle-covered muzzle, tearing his shirt.

'This has been in the sea.'

'Um. Yes. I regret the barnacles,' said Pontius. There goes another shirt, he thought.

'I do not know their provenance, I'm afraid. Been here time out of mind, you see. The other one is barnacle-free, I believe.' If the Captain were determined to go about embracing the ordnance, Pontius thought, a smoother muzzle might do a little less sartorial damage.

'I can tidy it up, make it beautiful again,' said Castello, peering into the gun's crusty muzzle in a way that made Pontius wince. 'But I fear it will never fire again.'

'*Fire?*' said Pontius in alarm. He had entertained no idea of actually firing the beastly things.

'My dear sir, why would we want to fire them?'

But Castello had moved on.

'This one,' he said, 'now this one could be restored to working order.' He peered down a second muzzle, to Pontius's discomfort. 'Yes, it will take work, of course, but quite possible.' Castello was already using his shirt cuff for some experimental polishing, Pontius noted, but the Captain was wholly absorbed and clearly happy.

'Pray, do not use your cuffs, Captain,' Pontius said hastily. 'The rust stains will never come out. I will fetch you an old cloth. Or a chisel. Or whatever you require.'

But Castello was only half-listening. He had danced round behind the second cannon and was looking along the barrel, now using both cuffs for extra polishing power.

'Good. Very good. Oh, a chisel. Yes please, Reverend, perhaps several. And a hammer. And a small mountain of cloths if you would.'

Pontius wasn't sure if he had achieved his objective or not. The look in Castello's eye was bordering on the obsessive. In any case, he called over a small boy and asked him to run up as fast as ever he could to Ferro the blacksmith and beg the loan of a hammer and chisel. That would take a little time, so Pontius bowed to Castello, who took no notice at all, and then took himself off to one of the fishermen's cottages to ask for a couple of cloths. He hoped he might find them before the shirt was irretrievably ruined.

In his heart, Pontius was content: Castello had not said another word about leaving the island, and that made the Reverend very happy.

Message on a Bottom

After a fine start that summer it had been a season of alternating broiling heat and heavy gales. The Reverend Pontius had feared for his roof at times, and his sanity at others. "Unhelpful weather", the Larus people called it.

After two days of one of these howling gales, the Reverend was polishing his pews, quite unnecessarily since he'd cleaned them the previous day—anything to avoid going outside, in truth—when the chapel door flew open.

'Come in, come in, whoever you are,' wailed Pontius, 'and close the door behind you. You're making the dust fly.'

The visitor was Ligo the fisherman, more than a little windswept, and looking a tad sheepish.

'Good day to you, Reverend. I wonder ... that is ... perhaps ...'

'Yes, yes,' said Pontius, chasing dust motes, 'spit it out, man.'

'I ... well ...' said Ligo, hat in hand, 'I've been looking at the merman's boat, the ship's boat he came in, thought I might make a few repairs, while the gale's blowing.'

'About time, too,' Pontius muttered, as he wielded the duster. He had suggested, oh, weeks ago, months even, that the boat should be tidied up and put to good use for the benefit of the community. The people had been reluctant to touch it, thinking the craft might have slightly magical properties what with it having a merman on board. Pontius had suspected at the time that they'd simply put it somewhere out of sight and forget it, and it seemed he had been right. Ligo had certainly taken a long while to start making repairs.

'And what condition do you find the boat in, Master Ligo?'

'Ah, sir ...well ... pretty good,' said Ligo, obviously uneasy.

Would the fellow ever come to the point? Pontius wondered. He feared that it would go on for hours, so he put down the duster and fixed Ligo with a penetrating stare.

'So, your difficulty is? Is there a difficulty?'

'Well, Reverend, there is writing on it. The boat, I mean. I thought maybe it tells what ship it belonged to. Might help jog the merman's ... I mean Captain Castello's memory, y'see.'

Pontius had his mouth open to say 'Don't bother me with damn silly ideas', and then had to shut it again. This was actually a very sensible idea.

'Well,' he said, 'I know you can read, Master Ligo, I taught you myself. What does it say?'

'Well, Reverend, that's just the difficulty, so to speak. It's writing, but not any sort I ever saw. Can't make it out, sir. Will you come and look at it?'

Pontius wondered why these things always turned up in the middle of a gale. But he truly wanted to see this mysterious writing for himself, so he heaved a sigh, put away the duster, fetched a hat and coat, and set off down the hill with Ligo loping alongside. As he had suspected, the boat had been left in a secluded corner, covered over with a bit of sailcloth.

'Here ...you see ... Reverend,' Ligo was pointing, '...under the cloth... look.'

There was definitely some obscure lettering on the boat's bottom. Pontius wondered why he hadn't noticed it before.

'I see it,' he said, rubbing sand and salt off the wood. 'That is the last letter, I think. A very old-fashioned script, but I believe that is a letter N.'

'Oh,' said Ligo, stepping back. 'Perhaps it says "Merman". That ends with a letter N.'

'Hmm,' said Pontius, squinting and trying to uncover the second-last letter. 'I think this one is an A.'

'Oh, it *does* say "Merman"!' said Ligo, now convinced and fearful.

'He's *not* a merman. How many times do I have to tell you?' Pontius was scraping away at the third-last letter. 'Anyway, look ... this one is an I, so it can't say "Merman", can it?'

'That is a relief, Reverend,' said Ligo, relaxing a little. 'So what *does* it say?'

'If you'll just let me finish, I'll tell you,' said Pontius.

Was this going to be helpful, or another disappointment? One by one the letters appeared, until the whole word became clear.

'It says "Guardian",' said Pontius, at last. '

'Oh.' Ligo backed away again.

'Is that a ship's name, d'ye think, Reverend?'

'It could be,' said Pontius, backing away a bit himself.

'Or perhaps it's a message.'

Having had experience of written messages from the Spirit of the Sea, Pontius was doubtful. He had never spoken to anyone about the words scrawled on his icy window, in the dust on the pews, or the item added to his own to-do list all those years ago. But they were certainly unexplained, and they had ultimately brought him to Larus. Could something similar have happened to Captain Castello?

The simple explanation of the writing on the boat was that it was the name of the ship it had belonged to. Why should a ship not bear the name *Guardian*, after all? Perfectly possible. But Pontius had to admit it was a striking coincidence that anything bearing that name should wash up on Larus, where that word had such particular significance. It was also very much the *modus operandi* of the Spirit of the Sea. *If* he admitted the existence of that deity. Which he didn't. Of course.

Pontius thought this over anxiously. It was imperative that he should tell Captain Castello about it as soon as possible, and preferably before he should receive a garbled version from somebody else. The story would be all over the island in no time, he knew, despite having asked Ligo to be discreet. There was no keeping a secret on Larus, not for long.

Castello had been polishing the cannon, and that was where Pontius found him.

'Good day, good day to you!' said Pontius, puffing with the effort of walking. 'All alone, Captain?'

'Haven't seen a living soul all morning, Reverend,' said Castello, unrolling his sleeves. 'And good day to you, too, sir.'

'Good,' said Pontius, relieved.

'I wanted to speak with you on a private matter. Or a public one. Possibly both.' Castello frowned.

'Eh? I don't quite understand you, Reverend.'

'Allow me to explain. Something has come to light which is a private matter for you, but owing to unavoidable and possibly scurrilous gossip, it will shortly be publicised to everyone on this isle. I should like to be the first to share it with you, in private, so you may hear an accurate account, not exaggerated gossip.'

Castello nodded and listened intently as Pontius recounted the tale of the writing on the boat.

'Well,' he said, 'it means nothing to me, I'm afraid, Reverend. Perhaps I did indeed come from a ship called the *Guardian*. Perfectly possible. But I have no recollection of it at all. I'll go and see it for myself, by and by. Perhaps it will remind me of something.'

A Glut of Guardians

As Pontius had feared, the story was soon all round the Isle. Not only the fact of the boat bearing the name *Guardian*, but also the exciting information that the Reverend thought it might be a message from the Spirit of the Sea.

'When shall I ever learn to keep my mouth shut in this place?' muttered Pontius, who most definitely did not wish to be associated with any messages from that deity. Privately, though, he wondered if Castello had indeed been sent to be a guardian of the Isle. Pontius very much wished the Captain to remain on Larus, but as a fellow guardian of the Isle? That was quite another matter.

But on an island where the written word was still considered more than slightly magical, whatever the Reverend said, gossip went on. It became ever more ridiculous, too, to Pontius' annoyance.

Some said a great ship named *Guardian* would come and take Castello away. Others said the ship and its crew would sweep away all the present guardians and take over the rule of Larus. No one said this in front of Rissa, since the lady ship-warden might not take kindly to the idea of being swept away, but it was widely held to be true. Still others said the whole thing was a warning to the guardians to mend their ways. No one said that to Rissa, either, but nonetheless it found its way into her scandalised ear and sent her steaming down to the chapel to confront Pontius.

'What do you propose to do about these outrageous rumours, Reverend?' she said, slamming the door so hard behind her that it made the bell all the way up in its tower give a surprised clang.

'*Me*?' said Pontius. 'Why me?'

'Because *you* found the lettering and made some remark about it being a message. It's all your fault.'

Pontius knew it was fruitless to point out that it had been Ligo the fisherman who found the writing and not himself. But he could not deny his careless remark about a message. He caved in.

'Very well, perhaps we should call a guardians' meeting.'

'A private meeting,' said Rissa. But both she and Pontius knew there was no such thing. Word always got around the island, and everyone would turn up. Guardians' meetings were rare events.

'As private as may be,' said Pontius, resignedly. He was not looking forward to it.

Rufus the Hermit practically never left his hovel on the west cliff. "Well," people said, "you could hardly expect him to go wandering about, not as a blind man now, could you?" He was their self-styled representative of the

Spirit of the Sea, and all he really needed to do was commune with the deity. Stumbling about the Isle didn't come into it.

So, the meeting was held on the west cliff for the convenience of the western guardian. Mistress Petronilla had been doubtful of Master Delphinus' attendance, given the distance he would need to walk, but said she would try to persuade him to come along. It had been a toss-up as to whether they held the meeting on the west cliff to ensure that Rufus took part, or on the quayside to guarantee the presence of the northern guardian. In the end, given that Rufus was generally more sensible, and that Master Delphinus' presence in his own head was unpredictable, they had settled for the west cliff.

Captain Castello was puzzled by the whole proceeding.

'It has nothing to do with me,' he said to Pontius. 'Island business. I should prefer to continue polishing the cannon if it's all the same to you.'

Pontius was less convinced of it being no concern of Castello's, but he felt it might be less distressing for his friend to stay out of it.

'Yes, indeed,' he said, reassuringly. 'There is no need for you to attend, not really. Your work is more important, my dear sir. I will tell you all about it when I return, never fear.'

As Pontius had expected, the guardians' meeting was far from private. Whole families trailed up to the west cliff, bringing their lunches and an air of festivity. Children scampered and old folks complained about the noise. Practically everyone was present, right down to one of Mrs Ferro's goats.

'There was no need to bring *that*, surely,' said Pontius.

'Her kid is due at any moment,' said Mrs Ferro, 'and I can't leave her unattended.'

Pontius resisted the temptation to point out that this was supposed to be a private meeting and that both Mrs Ferro *and* her goat might have stayed at home. The goat fixed him with a baleful eye and attempted to take a bite out of his sleeve.

'Get off!' said Pontius, backing away before his best frockcoat should suffer any damage.

Someone had brought a pennywhistle and began to play.

'They'll be dancing in a minute,' Pontius said, in despair. The chances of a sober and serious meeting were ebbing rapidly.

'Is everyone present? Where is the lady ship-warden?'

Someone said that Rissa was on her way.

'And Master Delphinus? Is he coming or not? Do let's get on.' Pontius was anxious to begin before the whole thing descended into farce.

A splash of scarlet moving along the cliff path showed that Rissa was about to join them.

'Thank goodness,' said Pontius, 'I am glad to see you, ma'am.' Just for once he was quite sincere.

Rissa inclined her head.

'Reverend. Why are all these people here?' Pontius shook his head and shrugged.

'You know how it is, ma'am. Word gets around. Can I tempt you to a seat on this convenient boulder?'

Rissa shook out her scarlet skirts and sat down. Pontius clapped his hands for silence.

'Very well, it doesn't seem that Master Delphinus is going to join us, so shall we make a start?' Tradition has it that three guardians is sufficient to convene a meeting, does it not?'

Everyone nodded. It was important that traditions be observed. Even the pennywhistle player had fallen silent.

Rissa stood up again.

'Can someone fetch the western guardian, please?'

Rufus the Hermit was escorted out of his hovel and brought to stand alongside Rissa and Pontius. It wasn't often the guardians stood together like this, and Pontius sensed an air of solidarity that he found rather comforting. Rissa and Rufus settled on adjoining boulders.

'With all respect to my colleagues,' Pontius said, bowing to them, 'I will explain the purpose of this meeting. You will be aware that the merman's boat—that is, Captain Castello's boat—was found to have something written upon it. Most of you will have seen it for yourselves. You will also know that the word written upon the boat is *Guardian* in an antique script. We are here to discuss the meaning, if any, of this and to put a stop to the ridiculous rumours that are circulating.'

Pontius knew the islanders dearly loved a ridiculous rumour, it gave them something to think about and they would be reluctant to give up on one. But it had to be done.

'My own opinion, if I may, Colleagues,' Pontius paused to glance at Rissa and Rufus, who inclined their heads graciously.

'I have consulted with Captain Castello, and he still has no recollection of how he came to be in the boat, so he is unable to shed any light on the matter. The name *Guardian* means nothing to him. My own opinion is that it is all the merest coincidence. The boat must have belonged to a ship named *Guardian,* as chance would have it.

Simple as that. Perhaps the lady ship-warden might like to tell us her thoughts?'

Pontius sat down on another boulder, a particularly uncomfortable one, and hoped the other guardians would keep their comments brief.

Rissa stood up and made a fuss of arranging her voluminous skirts.

'Thank you,' she said. 'I have heard some of these ridiculous rumours, and I agree with the Reverend.' Wonders will never cease, thought Pontius.

'It is the name of a ship and nothing more.' Rissa went on.

'Suggestions that it indicates this Captain Castello person was sent to us as a new guardian of the Isle are nonsense. Balderdash,' she added for emphasis. 'He is, in any case, clearly not a fit person for high office. He is at this moment too busy *polishing a cannon*, if you please, to attend this meeting.' She spat this out with obvious disgust.

Pontius was stung at this injustice and jumped up to say that he, himself, had advised Castello not to come to the meeting. Rissa shushed him, and he sat down again on the lumpy boulder, silenced.

'It is the name of a ship,' she said again, 'and let that be an end to it. What do you think, western guardian?' she asked, turning to Rufus the Hermit. 'And be quick about it. *I* have work to do, even if no one else does.'

Rufus stood and gazed towards the sea for long moments, quite unhurried, making Pontius and Rissa tap their feet in impatience. Trust him to make a meal of it, Pontius thought. A surreptitious glance at Rissa showed him she was thinking much the same thing. That's *twice* we've been in agreement today, Pontius thought.

'It is perfectly clear to the meanest intellect,' said Rufus, 'that the writing on the boat is a message from the Spirit of the Sea. It is not a ship's name; it is a description of the boat's contents. He has been sent to us by the spirit as a guardian of the Isle. Simple as that.'

Supercilious old fool, thought Pontius, bristling.

'The name of a ship would be a far more rational explanation ...'

'That's right,' said Rissa, 'Rational ...'

'Rubbish,' said Rufus. 'He is our new guardian.'

'But ...' Pontius was floundering in the face of this illogical certainty. 'We already have four guardians. Why would we be sent another? We don't require one.'

'No, we don't,' said Rissa, 'certainly not ...'

'That's what you two think,' said Rufus, tapping his nose in a very irritating way.

Pontius hesitated. He had spent most of his time on Larus pooh-poohing the Spirit of the Sea and promoting his own chosen deity, the Spirit of the Sky, with somewhat mixed results. But he also knew that he himself had been *called* to Larus, and though he resisted the idea, he privately admitted that the call had probably come from the Spirit of the Sea. It had certainly proved irresistible. The people believed the Spirit of the Sea provided a new guardian whenever one was needed. He himself had felt that call when there was a vacancy.

But there was no vacancy now. So, even if you believed it, which Pontius told himself he didn't, why would the spirit send them a spare guardian?

Pontius found his voice.

'But another guardian is extraneous ... superfluous ... unnecessary ... excess to requirements ...' He had run out of synonyms.

'Pointless,' said Rissa, who hadn't.

'Useless ... futile. And even if we did need one, it wouldn't be that Castello. Unsuitable ... unfitting ... inappropriate. Complete nincompoop.'

Pontius felt the need to defend his friend but didn't want to support the notion that he was a possible extra guardian of the Isle. The contradiction made him huff and then fall quiet.

'I don't think ...' But nobody ever found out what it was the Reverend Pontius didn't think. Everyone's attention was diverted by a small procession making its way very slowly indeed along the cliff path.

'Why,' somebody called out, 'It's Mistress Petronilla. She's brought

Master Delphinus to the meeting after all!'

There was a long delay as people rushed to assist their northern guardian before he slipped off the perilous path, and the pennywhistle man started up an encouraging tune while they waited.

'We'll never get done with this,' muttered Pontius. 'We'll be here all day at this rate. Why couldn't he just send a messenger instead of staggering all the way up here, silly old fool?'

Rissa looked equally cross, but Rufus the Hermit retained his air of smug serenity throughout. *He knew*, Pontius thought, he knew Delphinus was coming, and said nothing. He was tempted to give Rufus a piece of his mind. But perhaps not in front of the whole island. Something to look forward to at a later date, he thought, thoroughly enjoying the wicked intent, man of the cloth or not.

Pontius called Ligo the fisherman over.

'Perhaps you and your brother could carry Master Delphinus up here, if you would. Otherwise, we'll be here for the week.'

'Aye, sir, we could,' said Ligo. 'Lineus, give me a hand.'

Soon Master Delphinus, resplendent in his startling suit of yellow, was seated on a boulder, with his daughter at hand to provide assistance.

'My father has an announcement to make,' she said. 'Come along now, Dada, you remember what you wished to tell everyone, don't you?'

'Do I?' said Master Delphinus, looking puzzled.

'Yes, of course you do. You were going to say that you have reached a great age, weren't you?'

'Great age. Oh, yes,' said Master Delphinus, but then ran out of steam and paused again.

'And that you have star-gazed for the benefit of the Isle all these years,' prompted Mistress Petronilla.

'Star-gazed, I have,' said Master Delphinus, and stopped again.

'Let him speak for himself!' somebody yelled.

'We'll never get finished if we do that,' Pontius said. 'Mistress Petronilla, please continue.'

'Thank you, Reverend. Now, Dada, you were going to say ...'

Master Delphinus looked as if he had no idea what he was going to say but was quite cheerful at the prospect anyway.

'Going to say ...'

'You were going to say you had earned a rest. Time to take your ease.'

'My ease!' said Master Delphinus, 'Yes indeed.' And then lost the thread again.

'You were going to announce your well-earned retirement, Dada. Please try to say it.' Even Mistress Petronilla, a woman of boundless patience, was reaching the end of her tether.

'Try to say it. Retirement! Aha!' said Master Delphinus, clapping his hands in a flurry of golden-yellow cuffs.

'I shall retire! Now!'

'Just so,' said Rufus.

'Um ... well deserved, I'm sure,' said Rissa.

'Ye gods!' said Pontius.

'Baah!' said Mrs Ferro's goat, and promptly went into labour.

16

Barnacles Speak Louder than Words

The guardians' meeting had ended in chaos, with Mrs Ferro screaming for help and everyone crowding round anxious to provide the very best goat-birthing advice. The Reverend Pontius had called for order and been completely ignored, before admitting defeat.

In the end he had returned to Rissa and Rufus to recommend reconvening later. Rissa had tutted, but accepted she couldn't compete with a gravid nanny-goat on this occasion and had stalked off with a grand swishing of scarlet skirts. Pontius had escorted Rufus the Hermit back to his hovel.

'Told you so,' said Rufus. Pontius huffed. If there was one thing that was more annoying than someone being smug, it was their being right, too.

Finally, he had detailed Ligo to see Master Delphinus safely back down the hill. Duty done, he thought resignedly, and made his way back to the chapel.

The goat had indulged herself in a long labour, and it was the early hours of the following day before she was delivered of two bonny kids.

'I trust Mrs Ferro has no more of her goats in a state of advanced pregnancy,' Pontius grumbled.

'Such a fiasco!'

'Indeed,' said Rissa, who had come down to the chapel to agree a time for a new meeting. 'A complete waste of time it was.'

They were treading carefully round each other, neither choosing to mention that Master Delphinus' shock announcement had put a completely different complexion on things. Pontius and Rissa had both argued that the name on the boat was coincidental, indeed it must be, since they had no need of a new guardian. That argument had now evaporated, and Rufus' insistence that Castello had been labelled as a replacement guardian now looked alarmingly logical. Pontius was concerned that the deeply modest Castello would be scared off by the whole thing.

'We must continue the meeting,' said Rissa.

'We must, ma'am, and as a politeness to Master Delphinus I think we must meet on the quayside. I will not have the old gentleman carried up the cliff path again.'

Rissa nodded.

'I will, however,' Pontius went on, 'have Rufus the Hermit hauled bodily down to the quay whether the old fool likes it or not. We three must be present to form a guardians' meeting now that Master Delphinus has resigned.'

By the middle of that afternoon, word had gone around that a new private meeting was planned, and naturally everybody came along for the event. Rufus the Hermit had been conveyed from the west cliff in a handcart, complaining all the way, and goats had been expressly banned from attending.

Pontius had purposely not said much to Captain Castello, except that Master Delphinus was now an ex-guardian. Castello had asked nothing and taken himself off early to continue his work on the cannon. So, when the meeting began on the quayside, Castello wasn't far away and Pontius was acutely aware that his friend could probably hear most of what was said.

Rufus, clearly ruffled and with bits of straw stuck in his grubby robes, got in first.

'As I was saying before we were so rudely interrupted, the merman has been sent to us as a replacement guardian. We should accept him immediately as a gift from the Spirit of the Sea. Now take me back to the west cliff. I have important sea-communing duties to attend to.'

Pontius glanced at Captain Castello, further along the quay, and saw that he had stopped polishing and was looking alarmed. The hermit's voice was thin and wispy, but it had a surprising carrying quality. Dash it all,

Pontius thought, they'll frighten him to death. *He'll leave us.*

'Let us not be hasty,' he said, hoping his clergyman's voice carried equally far. 'After all, we do not know whether the merman, that is, Captain Castello, would wish to accept the position.'

'But he was labelled by the spirit,' someone said. 'Y'can't ignore that. No more can he.'

'Why don't we ask him?' Rissa took charge. 'He's just nearby. Fetch him over, Reverend.'

There was no arguing with her, and Pontius walked down the quay to Castello.

'Come along, friend,' he said, as encouragingly as he could.

'What should I say?' said Castello, looking terrified.

'The Spirit of the Sky will guide you.' It was the Reverend's standard advice in tricky situations.

'I'm not sure the Spirit's at home,' said Castello. But he allowed Pontius to propel him over to the meeting anyway.

'Go on, sir, do,' said Pontius, nudging the Captain in the ribs.

'I ... um ... there are barnacles on the cannon.' Castello was badly flustered at this sudden need for public speaking, and out of his depth, too. 'Difficult to remove them ... will probably never fire again.'

What? The crowd were silent. They had not called him in to discuss barnacle incrustations.

Rissa took charge again.

'Rufus the Hermit says the Spirit of the Sea has marked you as our new guardian. What d'you say to that?'

Castello looked as uneasy as any marked man rightly could.

'Oh,' he said. 'I don't know ...'

'Sir, sir!' A small boy was pushing through the crowd.

'Come and see what's happened, Mr Reverend, sir!'

Pontius was grabbed by the sleeve and tugged towards the cannon.

'What is it? I'm busy,' he protested, trying to brush the child off.

'Oh.'

Every barnacle had suddenly vanished from the gun's ancient muzzle, except for a neat grouping forming a legible word. *Guardian.* Everyone else had caught up and was gazing in awe.

'Tis a message from the spirit, sure 'nough.'

'It's the Captain's gun. He's to be our new guardian. Plain as the nose on your face, it is.'

'How many times do I have to tell you?' said an impatient voice in Pontius' ear. But when he turned to reply, there was no one there.

Of course there wasn't.

'Oh,' said Pontius, again. It was the best he could manage.

It had taken Captain Castello a long while to come round to the idea, but at last he had graciously accepted the position of northern guardian, Isle of Larus, to the great joy of all the people.

'They have such faith in me, in my ability to do this properly,' he said to Pontius. 'Far more than I have in myself.'

'My dear sir,' said Pontius, smiling, 'I felt just the same.

Guardianship is something you ease your way into, one step at a time. You will find your own way; I am sure of it. You are still a young man. There is plenty of time.'

'I wish I had your confidence, Reverend.' Castello looked worried, as he often did these days, Pontius noted.

Castello had now moved, by popular demand, into the room that was all that remained of the old castle, where he had spent the first part of his recovery. The people had all contributed household items and helped him fix the leaky roof. It wasn't exactly comfortable, but it was an adequate bachelor residence, and the Captain was entirely content with living next door to a pair of cannon.

He had left the barnacles forming the name *Guardian* on the old cannon's muzzle.

'Not a bad name for a gun really, is it?' he said. 'I am thinking of naming the other one. Any ideas, Reverend?'

Pontius had no idea guns could have names, but he wasn't about to argue it out. He almost suggested naming it *Rissa*, since it was dangerous to get in its way. And loud, too. But he thought better of it. Their southern guardian was very unlikely to appreciate the joke. Instead, he said, 'Well, if you think it requires a name ... but I beg you not to choose anything aggressive. We welcome visitors to Larus, do we not?'

'Very well,' said Castello, thinking. 'How about *Bulwark*? That is more defensive. And solid.'

Pontius nodded. It was as good as any name, if a cannon really needed one.

'Now, sir,' he said, 'come along with me. I have left something at Master Delphinus' house.'

Castello was curious.

'You have mislaid something, Reverend?'

'No,' said Pontius as they walked.

'Do you remember the hatchet-faced sea captain? Master ... Hixmux?'

'Huxmix, I think,' said Castello. 'I didn't meet him, but I heard about him. What of him?'

'Well, he had many things for sale, you recall, and I bought some shirts from him. I also ... bought something else. A gift for you.'

'A gift?' cried Castello, 'for me?'

'Yes, and I hope you will like it. Mistress Petronilla? May I have my package, please? There, sir. That is for you.'

Castello took the package and opened it. Inside was a military uniform.

'It is a little worn and shabby, I'm afraid,' said Pontius, 'an everyday uniform. Goodness knows where Master Huxmix acquired it, but I saw it and I thought of you. I confess I had put it aside until I was sure you would be staying with us.'

'It is quite wonderful,' said Castello, slipping the jacket on. 'The finest gift I ever had. I thank you with all my heart, Reverend. It is a little big, but I can adjust it quite easily. I can sew, you know.'

'I know,' said Pontius. 'Off you go now and search out a needle and thread.'

Epilogue

The Reverend Pontius and his friend Captain Castello, now resplendent in his new uniform, stood together in companionable silence, watching the sea crashing into the shingle.

'It has nearly all gone,' said Castello. 'Only the sails are left. I had thought they would disappear first.'

He was talking about the ship of the sky. Little by little, the islanders had dismantled it and it had swiftly become part of the fabric of Larus.

'Nothing much goes to waste here,' observed Pontius, 'however strange it might be.'

Indeed, a chunk of it was now acting as a very serviceable doorstop in the chapel.

'I had wondered,' said Castello, 'whether we might construct a sort of windmill from those sails, if they are not too frail. I shall look into it. A windmill could be useful, don't you think?'

It pleased Pontius very much to hear the Captain refer to the future. A future on Larus, that is.

'I have every confidence you will find a way to do it. You have a true genius with practical things. Just look at the improvements to my bell! Look at Master Delphinus' book! And the beautiful work you have done with the island's cannon. Everyone agrees you are a fine and useful addition to the community.' Was that going too far, Pontius wondered?

Castello cast his eyes downwards modestly.

'Hmm,' he said, and then changed the subject, as Pontius had known he would. 'But you know, Reverend, there are still many things that puzzle me. I cannot make out the materials that ship of the sky was built from. I do not recognise many of them at all. And the true purpose of its component parts is a great mystery.'

Pontius looked unconcerned.

'There are many things you do not recall, Brother. Perhaps you will remember them all in good time.'

Castello turned to look the Reverend in the face. He had never called him 'Brother' before. But the Captain liked it and put on a shy smile.

'Perhaps I shall.'

No one on Larus, except Captain Castello, had thought to question the origin of the ship of the sky. It was simply a gift from the spirit and that was that. Even the Reverend Pontius, offcomer though he was, had been on the Isle long enough to think more like the inhabitants than he might have realised. Besides, there were more important things to consider.

The island had gained a new guardian, the Reverend had gained a friend, and the Captain had gained a purpose in life. But maybe, just maybe, some other world—perhaps yours and mine, dear reader—had lost a communications satellite hijacked by a mischievous spirit.

'We can never know,' said Pontius, entirely oblivious to such possibilities, 'what the spirit may send us next.' It was just as well, for the good Reverend's peace of mind, that he knew nothing of the trials the future held for them all on the merry Isle of Larus.

THE END

OTHER TITLES BY KATHY SHARP

QUIRKY TALES SERIES:

978-1-914071-00-3 The Herbarium
978-1-914071-02-7 The Chesil Apothecary
978-1-914071-45-4 Dropwort Hall

ISLE OF LARUS SERIES:

978-1-914071-72-0 Call of the Merry Isle
978-1-916756-03-8 The Merman

Milton Keynes UK
Ingram Content Group UK Ltd.
UKHW020318031123
431651UK00011B/80